"I'll not join you in your wicked schemes!"

Cathleen told Lanty angrily. "Give me the will now and I'll forget you had it. I can't say fairer than that."

"You can say a lot fairer," Lanty shouted. "And you're not getting off this island until you do!"

Before she realized his intentions, he had turned, crashing his way through the undergrowth.

"Lanty!" she called breathlessly, racing after him. But by the time she reached the water's edge the boat had left the shore.

"Come back here!" she called frantically.

He laughed unpleasantly. "Not until you sign our agreement. Maybe I'll come back in the morning," he shouted. "Perhaps a night with the ghosts of Black Island will bring you to your senses."

ELIZABETH HOY

is also author of the
following title in the
HARLEQUIN CLASSIC LIBRARY

DO SOMETHING DANGEROUS

When You Have Found Me

ELIZABETH HOY

Originally published as Harlequin Romance #526

HARLEQUIN
CLASSIC LIBRARY

TORONTO·LONDON·NEW YORK·AMSTERDAM
SYDNEY·HAMBURG·PARIS·STOCKHOLM

Original hardcover edition published by
Mills & Boon Limited 1951
ISBN 0-373-80010-X

Harlequin edition first published May 1960
Golden Harlequin Library edition, Volume XXXII,
published March 1973
Harlequin Classic Library edition published April 1980

Printed in Canada

CHAPTER ONE

THE CITY CLOCKS were chiming seven when Cathleen whisked that last letter out of her typewriter that hot July evening. Everyone else had gone home long ago and the offices of Gilmer & Co., Wholesale Importers, were silent, save for the whir of the vacuum cleaner Mrs. Chiddock, the cleaning lady, was using in old Mr. Gilmer's room. Cathleen was secretary to old Mr. Gilmer—a position her stepmother frequently pointed out to her she was very lucky to have obtained. But at twenty it is difficult to be consistently grateful for the privilege of typing balance sheets and company reports and long dull letters eight hours a day, five days a week.

Cramming the cover on the typewriter Cathleen leaned back with a sigh of exultation, hardly able to believe that four blissful weeks would elapse before she lifted that cover off again. Her eyes grew dreamy—very blue eyes, fringed with their thick black lashes, as Irish as the spelling of her name. Boglands she was seeing now, pansy dark under a high, windy sky, mountains the color of passion flowers and a vast sheet of water flung down like a shield at their feet. That Connemara travel film, chanced upon on a wintry Saturday afternoon, that had been the beginning of everything . . . Joan Kent saying over the teacups afterward, "Why don't we go to Ireland for our holiday this summer, Cath? Just the two of us. Shed our respective families and do a bit of sightseeing on our own?"

Even now Cathleen could remember the swift leap of her pulses . . . the ache, like a knot of unshed tears that had tightened in her throat; all the strange undefinable emotions the film had roused, surging up in such an overwhelming wave that she couldn't answer Joan. Ireland! The shadow land of her lonely childish imaginings. How often she had tried to picture the circumstances that might one day lead her there—but it had never occurred to her that it could come about as simply as this.

"That lovely lake with the mountains all around it," Joan had gone on. "Lough Osborne, wasn't it?" With a sense of destiny closing in on her Cathleen had nodded—still speechless. The mother she had never known had been an Osborne—Sheila FitzOsborne of Castle Osborne. How misleadingly grandiloquent that would sound spoken across the humble tea-shop table! And Joan would inevitably ask questions it wouldn't be easy to answer. Simpler to let her keep on with her busy planning, agreeing here, dropping a suggestion there. So that later, when they visited the travel agency's office, it could seem to be by the purest chance that the map spread out for their examination showed, once again, if more prosaically than in the film, the great loch with its famous fishing village of Osbornestown.

Even then Cathleen had found herself unable to speak of her dead mother's ancestors. The bright fantasies she had woven around that legendary figure were too precious, too intangible, to be shared with Joan Kent. All her young life Cathleen had hidden her secret loneliness in her heart—as motherless children do—guarding her little sanctuary of grief rigidly from her bustling, sensible stepmother and from the noisy brood of half brothers and sisters with whom she had never quite fitted in. And her father, in whom she might have confided, hadn't encouraged her in what had, no doubt, seemed to him to be a tendency toward unwholesome brooding. In that last memorable talk before his death he had made it so clear to her that not only her mother, but all that her mother had been, was lost in a past that could have no effect on her now. She was Cathleen

Trenton of Petunia Road; born and bred in a middle-class London suburb. The shadowy FitzOsbornes were nothing to her, less than nothing. "A dwindling line," he had dismissed them. "Your mother's death would leave only old Lady FitzOsborne, who does not know of your existence and would have nothing to do with you if she did . . . nor would I wish it any other way. There could be no happiness for you in any contact with the proud and bitter woman who broke your mother's heart . . . wrecked her young life."

Remembering now on this July evening the grim implacability of his tone, Cathleen glanced a little guiltily across the office at her suitcase all neatly labeled for the Angler's Hotel, Osbornestown, Lough Osborne. Was she being disloyal to her father's wishes in making this trip to the place of her mother's girlhood? But surely that was an unnecessarily morbid idea! The whole thing had come about almost by accident. She was simply going to spend her summer holiday in Connemara with her best friend, Joan Kent, climbing hills and swimming in the lough and eating the lavish Irish meals that were attracting so many holidaymakers from the austerity of post-war England.

As for Castle Osborne, her father had carefully wiped out any lingering notion of romance she might have had of that ancestral home. Ireland, he had pointed out on one of the rare occasions when she had persuaded him to talk of that fabulous land, was full of so-called "castles" that weren't really castles at all; decaying eighteenth-century mansions long since—where they had survived the upheavals of civil war—taken over by the new government to be used as hotels or schools. So that really it was silly to get all steamed up about a trip that would provide no more than the vaguest of associations.

Standing up, Cathleen stretched her cramped limbs, savoring the moment's relaxation, letting the office and all that it stood for slip away from her like a hampering garment discarded. In the wall mirror over the old-fashioned grate she could see herself, tall and young and very slender, her lifted arms like wings poised for flight, her face under its cloud of dark curls lit by the moment's bright expectancy, her burning blue eyes looking back at her filled with the eager questioning of youth.

With a clatter of broom handles and pails Mrs. Chiddock emerged from Mr. Gilmer's room. "You plannin' to spend the night here?" she inquired in an aggrieved tone.

"I'm just going, Mrs. Chiddock!" Hurriedly Cathleen shrugged herself into her new, fleecy travel coat and was out in the corridor making for the elevator when the clamor of the office telephone halted her. Running back to answer it she tried not to remember how unlucky it is supposed to be to turn back at the beginning of a journey!

It was Joan Kent calling, her voice shrill with urgency. "Cathleen? Oh, it *is* you! Thank heavens I've caught you . . . I was hoping you'd still be at the office clearing up. . . ." The words poured out then faster and faster and, listening in horror, Cathleen held the receiver so tightly that her knuckles ached. Joan couldn't meet her at Euston Station in an hour's time—as they'd planned. Joan couldn't come to Ireland! Her mother had had an accident, falling on the stairs fracturing a hip joint. "There's no bed available at the local hospital and we can't even get a nurse . . ." the frenzied voice ran on.

Pity for Joan's plight and Mrs. Kent's pain were swamped for a moment in sheer agonizing disappointment.

"But I can't possibly go without you!" Cathleen cried in panic.

"I never heard anything so silly in my life! You've *got* to go," Joan shrilled back in the last stages of exasperation. "The Travelways people will look after you all through the journey— and there's our room booked at the hotel where that nice Mrs. Callaghan who wrote so kindly will be expecting us. We can't *both* let her down. I'm sure she'll make you feel at home, and you'll probably soon find friends among the other guests. Irish hotels aren't likely to be stiff and starchy. Maybe I'll even be able to join you later . . . if I can find a nurse for mother. . . .''

"Oh, Joan, you think that's likely?"

"You can bet I'll get over to you if it's humanly possible. And now for heaven's sake push off, Cath, or you'll be missing your train. Let me know how you get on. Bye!" The line went dead.

With legs that weren't quite steady Cathleen tottered out into the corridor once more. Running down the familiar steps of the subway station she might have taken out her season ticket and headed straight for home—only that home was shut up, the family having departed for Bognor that morning. She could, of course, creep after them in cowardly surrender, but the thought of the Crantons stiffened her faltering spirit—next-door neighbors who'd teamed up with the Trentons this year, mainly, Cathleen suspected, because Len Cranton, the only son, had worked it that way, foreseeing a whole month of sunbathing and swimming and dancing—with herself. Poor Len, who was so patiently persistent and so good . . . and so boring, making her suffer endless pangs of guilt because she couldn't quite feel about him the way he felt about her. Though why she *didn't* fall in love with his admirable qualities she couldn't understand. He was so exactly the type of young man all the girls in Petunia Road ended up by marrying contentedly. "You'll go farther and fare worse," her disapproving stepmother had warned.

Well, I am going farther, Cathleen thought now in bright defiance. "Euston, please," she said firmly to the booking clerk—and the dye was cast.

After that it was all increasingly simple. There in the big cavernous terminus was the man from Travelways to guide her to her reserved seat. A cabin had been booked for her on the boat, and at Kingstown on the Irish side another Travelways official would be waiting to pilot her to the train that would take her across Ireland. So she couldn't get lost if she tried.

Feeling rather like a parcel in the hands of an extremely efficient postal service, she settled down to enjoy the bustle of departure all around her. It was as though Ireland had come to meet her, she thought on a wave of returning excitement. Everyone in the compartment and on the platform outside the compartment seemed to be Irish . . . making for home. Listening to the soft, quick, lilting voices, Cathleen felt her heart warm. As though she, too, were going home!

Doors slammed, whistles sounded; in the corridor at her side pandemonium broke out as a young man, carrying an amazing assortment of luggage, flung himself onto the moving train in a last-minute rush. An enormous young man in an extremely shabby tweed suit, he looked hot and tired and angry, dropping his burdens in a series of impatient thuds onto the corridor floor; a fat gunnysack, a bulging suitcase, a brand new fishing rod and a cat basket from which wails of distress emerged. Mopping his brow he glared witheringly and defiantly at the occupants of the crowded carriage—the look of a man who expects to be snubbed rather than welcomed, and is determined to brazen it out.

"There *is* a seat vacant," Cathleen murmured shyly, indicating Joan's empty corner opposite her own.

"But isn't it reserved?" the young man asked, eyeing with suspicion the Travelways label pinned to the gray upholstery.

"It was booked by a friend of mine who had to change her plans at the last moment. You're very welcome to it."

The young man made an indefinite sound that might have been an ungracious "Thanks!" and proceeded to pile his unwieldy luggage onto the already overcrowded rack. When, none too gently, he deposited the cat basket on top of the precariously placed gunnysack, Cathleen felt the sinking sense of horror the contemplation of suffering animals invariably caused her. Surely he wasn't going to leave the poor frightened creature up there in the cramped basket all through the long night journey! A Siamese by the sound of it—those mournful, uncatlike cries with their half-human intonations. Everyone knew Siamese cats were at least twice as sensitive as the ordinary kind . . . besides, the basket wasn't safe on the rack, Cathleen tormented herself. At the first lurch of the train it would come toppling down on the young man's head. Which, of course, would serve him right . . . but wouldn't be very nice for the cat.

She glanced indignantly across the little space between them. What a lot of room he seemed to take up—his shoulders far too broad for the small space allotted to him by an optimistic railway, his legs so long that even though he had done his best to curl himself out of the way his knees jutted out alarmingly, leaving Cathleen almost no room to move. Continuing her scrutiny, she decided he might have been attractive if he weren't so untidy and so obviously in a bad temper. The way the thick dark hair grew in a peak on his forehead, the strong nose and jaw, the firm, well-cut mouth above the cleft chin, the stormy gray eyes under level brows; eyes that, looking up suddenly to catch her interested gaze, made the foolish color rise in her cheeks.

"It's that cat," she found herself blurting stupidly. "I can't bear to hear it crying. Aren't you going to let it out?"

"No," the young man returned curtly, unfolding an evening newspaper with a dismissing air. Cathleen's color deepened. What a boor he was! Her spirit stiffening, she decided she wasn't going to let him get away with it. Besides, she really was troubled about the cat. It sounded so lost and heartbroken.

She said with a firmness that belied her inward tremors, "It isn't going to be very pleasant for the occupants of this carriage if we've got to listen to that noise for the next four hours or so. If you would like to pass the basket down to me, I'll let the cat out . . . *and* look after it."

The newspaper went down with an exasperated rustle, gray eyes blazed. Everyone in the carriage was interested now, a middle-aged matron in a towering turban coming out strongly on Cathleen's side. "Indeed, then, the young girl is right," she pronounced in a rich and fruity brogue. " 'Tis a poor thing for the cat and for ourselves if it is to be bawling its head off across the width of England." The young man seemed to recognize defeat when he saw it. With a sigh that was half a groan of despair for the fussiness of all females, he stood up and jerked the basket from its perch, depositing it on Cathleen's lap.

"I'll just open it a little. I won't let her out right away," she promised, with a mixture of caution and sheer triumph.

"It's a 'he,' " the young man corrected crossly. "A pedigree Siamese kitten I was commissioned to bring home for my kid sister. If you let it loose in this train on your own head be it. It cost every penny of ten guineas and it's as savage as a young fox."

"The Lord save us!" the middle-aged woman gasped, and with fingers that trembled a little Cathleen unfastened the straps of the basket, aided by a long, slim brown paw that shot out to assist her. A small brown "mask" followed, lit by a pair of strangely human blue eyes. "The darling!" Cathleen cried, and forgetting all caution lifted the small, firm fawn-colored body to her shoulder. With a little crooning sound the kitten nestled in her neck, so grateful for release from the basket that it began to lick her cheek with a small, quick tongue.

"It's not savage at all!" she exulted.

The young man shrugged. "It almost bit the hand off myself, when I was fastening it into the basket," he retorted, his deep voice for the first time falling into the intonations of the prevailing brogue.

So he is Irish, Cathleen thought with a thrill of satisfaction she couldn't have accounted for. But of course he was Irish, every bone in his lean young body, every fold of his shabby homespun proclaimed it—so did the stormy gray eyes that flashed fire as she demanded, "Wouldn't *you* bite the hand off anyone who was cramming you into a horrible dark basket and carrying you away from your home?''

A flippant inquiry he did quite right to ignore, Cathleen decided—able to be magnanimous now that she had scored over him in the matter of the imprisoned cat. Fondling the trembling little animal, she murmured endearments into the beautifully ''pricked'' pedigree ears, until presently it curled up in her arms and went contentedly to sleep.

Peace fell on the carriage then. In one corner a gentle-eyed nun clicked rosary beads softly as she said her evening prayers; the middle-aged lady removed her turban and wrapped herself in an enveloping shawl; behind the now slackly held evening newspaper the young man's dark head began to nod in drowsiness. Soon Cathleen was the only wakeful one, listening to the subdued snoring of her fellow travelers and the rhythmic roar of wheels as the great express raced through the night. Easy now to study the strong, lean face opposite, defenseless in sleep. Those lines carved prematurely on the high, good brow, the grim set of the young mouth . . . the face of a man who had lived hard and endured the hardness with courage rather than resignation—a fighter to the last bone in his body. What was it he fought? Poverty perhaps. Those sensitive hands with their hint of breeding had done their share of manual toil by the look of them. Probably he was a farmer. Most men in Ireland were farmers, Cathleen concluded sweepingly, and with an unaccountable little sigh turned to peer out of the night-blackened window at her side. Somehow it didn't seem quite fair to stare at people when they were asleep and couldn't stare back. But again and again as the slow moments crawled by she found her glance returning to that flung-back, beautifully shaped head and stony profile . . . he had turned a little now, pillowing his cheek on the cushion where Joan's ticket dangled. Long legs sprawling out imprisoned her, so that she could not have moved without touching some part of them. Some touch of unconscious egotism in the young man's pose annoyed her. Impishly, in contrast, her thoughts produced Len Cranton—patient, self-effacing Len, who would never, sleeping or waking, have dared to take up so much of a railway carriage. And yet the recollection of his virtues, as usual, left her cold. You couldn't imagine *this* man hanging around unwanted after some girl, putting up with snubs, neglect.... But then you couldn't imagine him ever condescending to fall in love at all. Or could you? The quick color ran up in Cathleen's cheeks as finally she closed her eyes, shutting away deliberately now that limply unconscious form, and somehow remaining all the more tingl-ingly aware of it. There was something too intimate, faintly outrageous, about this jumble of snoring humanity boxed up in the hot, airless gloom. Night journeys, she decided, as the head of the plump matron came down on her shoulder, were curiously promiscuous affairs. And she had never traveled all through a night before—that was why she was so vividly alive to impressions; too interested to sleep as these more sensible people did.

But she was excited, strung up; this feeling of a journey through time rather than space. Behind her tensely shut, aching lids the odd illusion came back to her ... this going back through the years to find she knew not what—blue hills, a shining lough, an old gray house, perhaps, where a girl so like herself had long ago lived and dreamed. Disjointedly her thoughts drifted back over the fragmentary history that was all she knew. If her father had lived there were so many things she could have asked him, but he had died, an overworked general practitioner, during the war when she was a child. There had been so little time in the end for that halting sickbed conversa-tion when he had given her the FitzOsborne cross set with garnets and her mother's photograph. A girl with the same thickly lashed Irish eyes as herself, her white shoulders wreathed in folds of old-fashioned tulle.

"She was nineteen when I met her," the dying man's voice had whispered. "A broken child who came to me for healing after the death of her first husband, killed before her eyes taking a fence in a steeplechase . . . drunk then, as he had been since the day twelve months earlier when he married her. You are young to know these sordid details, Cathleen—but it is your own mother's story." And there were so many things, Cathleen reflected now, she would never know; the name and ancestors of her mother's first husband . . . had he, too, come from Lough Osborne? Had that tragically unwise love affair been the only reason for the upheaval that had ended in Lady FitzObsorne turning her daughter out of the house, refusing from that time to have any contact with her; even returning her letters unopened. There had been in that final circumstance for Cathleen a touch of cruelty, so cold, so absolute that she had, in clear and childish judgment, seen the guilt where it truly lay. It was her grandmother, not her mother who had been to blame in the quarrel that had thrown a girl of eighteen adrift upon the world with no one but a drunkard to turn to.

"So that old Lady FitzOsborne never knew of your mother's marriage to me the following year," her father had gone on that unforgettable night. "Nor . . . how happy we were . . . until the end, which came so soon!"

"Because I was born," Cathleen had whispered in young anguish.

"You were the light my Sheila left to me," her father had answered, and as long as she lived the warmth of those words would comfort her heart. Resting upon them now, she felt her taut nerves relax. Sleep came to her then, mindless, profound.

When she awoke with a start the train was pulling into a great hollow-sounding cavern, filled with the cold, salt breath of sea—Holyhead Pier. In the carriage, confusion reigned as the occupants struggled with luggage. Rubbing the sleep from her eyes Cathleen saw the kitten still curled on her lap—and looked around for its owner. He was already in the corridor, his gunny-sack on his back. More dead than alive, Cathleen staggered out to him. "Your Siamese," she said.

The young man swung around with a sharp "Good Lord!" as though he had forgotten all about that troublesome animal. Tucked in her fleecy travel coat, Cathleen drew the limp, warm little body closer, an odd, bleak emptiness filling her heart. It was simply, she assured herself, that she hated the thought of handing the kitten over to this most careless young man who would probably want to spend the hours of the voyage in the bar hobnobbing with cattle jobbers.

"Look here," she found herself offering, "I'll keep it, if you like. I've got a cabin and it can go on . . . er . . . lying down. I'm going to, myself."

Relief, and for the first time something like gratitude showed in the stormy gray eyes, though his cool, "That's very nice of you," had a faintly mocking sound, as though fussing over kittens was a silly feminine peculiarity for which he had little sympathy. He did, nevertheless, have the graciousness to pick up Cathleen's suitcase, adding it by some superhuman feat of juggling to the burdens he was already carrying; escorting her to the door of her cabin, where he left her with a kindly, "Sleep well, now—and if the cat is a nuisance hand it over to Joe, here; he's your steward and he'll look after you."

Shut up in the hot, enclosed space, however, Cathleen felt she didn't in the least want to sleep. It would have been much more fun to roam the great ship . . . her first ship! How romantic it had looked towering above the dark, water-lapped pier, painted white and gay with lights. A swift picture came to her of herself standing in the stern watching the wake of foam spread ghostly in the darkness—a tall tweed-clad figure at her elbow. Kilmoran, that was the young man's name it seemed. "Good evening, Mr. Kilmoran," Joe the deck steward had murmured just now with a flattering degree of deference in his tone. It was a name with a hint of clannish authority . . . a good name with family behind it; a family littered with thanes and earls stretching back to the days of the Anglo-Norman invasion, thought Cathleen, vaguely recalling her Irish history. Perhaps he wasn't a farmer after all—or only a farmer in some elegant way, breeding racehorses maybe, keeping stables full of hunters and valuable stud mares. Though whatever he was really couldn't matter. Once they got to Kingstown and she'd handed the kitten over she would in all probability never set eyes on the brusque and rather annoying Mr. Kilmoran again.

With an odd little sigh she turned to the mirror over the competently fitted washbasin and saw herself pink cheeked and very wide awake, her short curls blown into an unruly mop upon her brow, her blue eyes shining . . . like the eyes of a child at its first Christmas party! Sea voyages, she had been told, sent people a little mad—this slightly intoxicating movement of the floor beneath her feet, the sound of waves that surged and sucked as the ship increased its speed. Even the kitten seemed affected, rushing in wild excitement around the tiny room, uttering little cries of delight, climbing at last with the agility of a monkey into the swaying bunk, where when the motion became uncomfortably marked Cathleen gratefully joined it. There was perhaps something to be said for the cabin after all! It wasn't a smooth crossing, but lulled by the throb of distant engines Cathleen dozed a little, and it seemed no time at all before Joe put his head in at the door to say, ''We'll be in harbor in about half an hour, miss. Mr. Kilmoran sends his compliments and says if you'd care to join him in the saloon for breakfast he'd be very pleased. But if you'd rather have just a cup of tea in here . . .'' the boy ended; his deferential air for seasickness now, rather than for rank!

Surprised, disheveled, Cathleen tumbled from her bunk. ''I'll join Mr. Kilmoran, thanks, Joe.'' Did she say it just a little too eagerly? In the mirror she saw her cheeks crimson over as she tugged curls into place, dabbed powder on her small, straight nose, Joe hovering discreetly outside. Following him down endless, swaying corridors she found herself at last in a crowded dining saloon where lights paled in the dawn. If she had had secret visions of a quiet tête-à-tête meal she was to be disappointed. Kilmoran, rising to greet her, waved her to a place he had kept for her at a long table filled with red-faced men in the same nondescript homespun garments as himself. Loud-voiced, voluble, they roared at one another across the cruets and sauce bottles and glasses of foaming stout, shoveling away vigorously at the mountains of food piled on the plates before them. Cattle appeared to be their passion—a passion in which it seemed Kilmoran was only too glad to share. Animated, completely transformed, he told of the Agricultural Show he had traveled to England to visit, breaking off now and then to make sure Cathleen had her share of the huge platter of eggs and bacon he had ordered. Apart from these abstractedly polite gestures she might not have existed. So he *was* a farmer in spite of the aristocratic name. Wading gloomily through the most lavish breakfast she had seen in years, Cathleen wished she had accepted Joe's offered cup of tea. This meal, flung at her as a kind of payment for her care of the Siamese kitten was . . . almost an outrage. She would insist upon paying her share when the bill was presented. Not as much as one rind of bacon would she accept from this offhand young man!

Looking up she found the gray eyes regarding her with an odd intensity, as though he were really seeing her for the first time. "Anything worrying you?" he asked. There was a hint almost of long-established intimacy about the softly spoken, direct little question.

But, still ruffled, Cathleen murmured a stiff, "No."

"Those eggs all right?"

"Perfectly." She was not going to discuss the merits of a meal she was determined to buy for herself. His hostlike solicitude was wasted.

"Well, eat a good breakfast," he persisted. "It will be nine o'clock tonight before you get to the Angler's at Osbornestown, and you've a hard day's travel before you."

Her blue eyes widened, emptied suddenly of chagrin. "How did you find out I was going to Osbornestown?"

Amusement flashed in the lean, tanned face—like sudden sunshine aslant dark waters. How different . . . how human and appealing he could look when he smiled! He had seen the boldly printed label on her suitcase while they waited in the customs shed at Holyhead, he explained, and abandoned her then to fling himself once more into the argument over curd in calves that was in hot progress. A moment later a distantly felt cessation of movement announced the arrival at Kingstown Pier and there was a general scramble in which Cathleen's hurriedly made attempt to settle for her breakfast was met by an abstracted and rather annoyed, "It's paid for long ago. Run on now like a good girl and get me the cat . . . in its basket, mind!"

Bemusedly she found herself obeying the order, and after that it was no time at all before Mr. Kilmoran walked out of her life. His farewell was characteristic, the hint of mockery in the slow smile as he murmured his thanks for her help with the Siamese. "And listen to me!" The smile broadened into a mischievous grin. "Don't go letting yourself be too fond of cats . . . yet a while. Leave them to the old maids God created them for!"

Before she could think of a suitably withering retort to this sally he was gone, and a moment later she had been taken over by the Travelways official waiting to meet her. After that the journey seemed curiously flat—which was entirely, Cathleen assured herself, because she was tired from her broken night; the long wait in Dublin where it rained steadily and she felt cold, then the crawling progress across the dull central plain of Ireland in a train that seemed to stop at every station.

By the time she arrived at Osbornestown she had been traveling solidly for twenty-eight hours and had reached that state of fatigue when nothing seems quite real anymore. Standing on a strip of broken pavement she stared in bewilderment at the narrow-fronted shabby house that bore no resemblance to a hotel, though the driver of the bus that had brought her the last twenty miles of the way had told her that if it was the Angler's she wanted . . . this was it. Only the enormous stuffed pike grinning at her from a fanlight over the weathered door gave her the courage to lift the knocker. And how odd to have to knock! Hotels were usually wide open welcoming places . . . waiting to be walked into . . . eager to be walked into. Nervously she glanced down the empty street, silent and gray in the gathering darkness, the mountains black as thunder rising in menace where the scatter of small, mean houses came to an end. The faint sense of disillusion that so often lurks at the end of even the most successful journey became a wave of icy and engulfing loneliness. If only Joan had been here! Oh, it had been foolish to set out on this holiday alone. Supposing nobody ever answered this tightly shut inhospitable door!

Timidly she knocked again and almost at once heard bolts withdrawn and found herself face to face with a harassed boy in the white jacket of a bartender. "Is it the two ladies from the Travelways?" he asked, peering over Cathleen's shoulder—as though he were seeing poor Joan's ghost.

"Only one lady," Cathleen corrected. "My friend was unable to come at the last moment and asked me to say that she hopes the sudden cancellation will not inconvenience you. . . ."

"Ah, not at all, sure aren't we only too glad she is kept from us!" was the astonishing reply, delivered with fierce emphasis. "The pity of it is," the boy went on with an uneasy laugh, "that yourself didn't stay home along with her! But if ye'll step into the lounge there, I'll bring Mrs. Callaghan to ye."

Far from reassured by this odd welcome, Cathleen went nervously through the door indicated into a long brilliantly lighted room, unexpectedly large and opulent compared with the humble exterior of the hotel. Groups of extraordinarily dressed men and women thronged around a chromium-fitted bar at one end. Rubber wading boots topped · by oil-stained Windbreakers seemed to be the prevailing costume, irrespective of sex, though a gloss of sophistication burnished the women with their mascaraed lashes, overred lips and lacquered nails. Everybody seemed to know everybody else and Christian names were much in evidence.

Standing awkwardly apart from these convivial souls, feeling like a gate-crasher at some intimate family party, Cathleen caught references to casting and spinning, to wind drifts and something known as a ''sunk float,'' which seemed to be inspiring a good deal of animated discussion. Once more the sense of desolation returned. Why, oh why, had she come to this outlandish place? How would she bear it day after day, creeping around like an outcast in a world full of people who did nothing apparently but catch fish . . . and drink. With the utter hopelessness of the very young she wrote off her holiday at that moment as a lost and dismal enterprise. And it was just then the raucous and unmistakable cry of a Siamese came to her. The breed, it seemed, was fashionable in Ireland. Drifting without much interest in the direction of the cries, Cathleen saw a knot of children gathered around a deep settee on which a red-headed girl of about fourteen sat with a kitten on her lap—a kitten so like the little creature of last night's journeyings that Cathleen stared in astonishment.

''Sweet, isn't he?'' the girl said, catching her interested glance. ''My brother has just brought him from London for me.''

''So it *is* the kitten I nursed in the train!'' Cathleen brought out, with something like terror in her tone.

The girl's hazel green eyes lit up. ''Oh, it was *you?*'' she began in obvious pleasure. ''Randy said an awfully nice girl had mothered Yo-Yo all the way to Kingstown . . . and that you were coming here. In fact he told me to look out for you. He's gone home on my bike and I'm to take the car when Paddy Lenihan at the garage has it fixed. It went wrong because Randy drove it too hard coming from Kingstown. He always does.''

The implications of this hurriedly made speech were too unexpected to be assimilated at once; like hailstones striking a windowpane only to bounce off again, the series of crisp announcements flicked at Cathleen's bewildered consciousness. Randy! The Kilmoran man. He lived at Osbornestown. He had spoken of her—incredibly—as an ''awfully nice girl'' . . . and yet he'd driven home from the steamer without having the decency to offer her the lift that would have saved her that long, slow journey in a cross-country train.

''Miss Trenton from the Travelways, is it?'' a worried voice interrupted her musings, and turning, Cathleen found a plump woman in black surveying her. A work-worn hand shot out. ''I'm Mrs. Callaghan, and I'm delighted to see you, Miss Trenton, only that I'm in an awful fix. My brother Tim is after accepting about a dozen extra bookings for this week with no more idea than that cat there where we are going to put the people to sleep. I've a colonel in the bath at this minute . . . and another gentleman shaking down on the billiard table.''

''Oh!'' Cathleen gasped, in real terror this time. So this was the meaning of the doorman's vaporings. With visions of herself turned adrift in the empty street with its menacing mountains, her blue eyes widened.

''I'm all day scouring the village for somewhere that might take you,'' Mrs. Callaghan went on. ''But every bed in the place is let; it's always the same in the summer when the visitors are here for the fishing. Tim ought to have more sense, but he's that good-hearted the poor man, he doesn't like disappointing people, telling them we've no room for them . . . and now here you are after your long journey, and the truth is I don't know what I am going to do with you. There isn't a bus back to Dunbarragh until morning.''

''But I don't want to stay in Dunbarragh, I want to stay here,'' Cathleen began, her lips trembling, so stunned by the magnitude of her misfortune that she hardly heard the red-headed girl when she said quietly, ''You could come home with me.''

''Indeed, then, Miss Mollie, that same passed through my own mind,'' Mrs. Callaghan put in quickly. ''Only that herself will likely eat the face off you if you go bringing in strangers.''

''She needn't be a stranger . . . we can say she is a friend,'' Mollie returned calmly. ''Honestly,'' she repeated turning to Cathleen, ''you can come to us, if you like. You were so kind to Yo-Yo last night that it is quite true to say you are our friend.''

''You mean you take paying guests?'' Cathleen blurted in bewilderment.

''We did last year until herself got sick of having strangers around the place and threw them all out one morning. But she wouldn't mind you—especially if she thought you were a guest. It was having people pay that she hated.''

''But naturally I should pay . . . if I came,'' Cathleen added wildly, not at all sure that she wanted to be whisked away by this pixielike child into an unknown that included the moods of Mr. Randy Kilmoran.

The redhead nodded. ''You could pay kind of secretly . . . give it to Randy, on the quiet,'' she said. ''We've talked it over already, because he thought you might be stranded tonight.''

''How very kind of him!'' Cathleen murmured, more bewildered than ever.

''Not at all,'' Mollie returned graciously. ''Randy would do anything to get extra money for his new farm.''

''Oh!'' gasped Cathleen, rather as if she had had a wet rag slapped across her face.

''Well as long as Mr. Kilmoran told you you could take the

young lady, my mind is at ease,'' Mrs. Callaghan weighed in comfortably. ''If you could put her up even for a week itself, it would be a great boon to me.''

Cathleen opened her mouth to speak and shut it again with a strangling sound. She felt as though she were drowning in a rising tide of circumstance too strong for her. And she was desperately tired. She had to find *somewhere* to lay her head tonight.

''It's very kind of you, Miss Kilmoran,'' she managed to bring out at last—without much enthusiasm.

After that everything seemed to become very confused—like an indefinite but worrying dream. That endless drive through the pitch dark lanes; Mollie urging the old car along at top speed, saying at intervals, ''If the police stop us, I'm done. I'm too young to have a license though I've been driving since I was thirteen.''

Bouncing on a springless seat Cathleen clutched the worn-out and half-demented Yo-Yo in her arms, longing now only for her safe, comfortable bed in Petunia Road . . . longing for Joan who would never have become involved in a crazy adventure like this . . . dreading her arrival at the Kilmoran abode so intensely that she felt quite sick. And Mollie's candid chatter did nothing to help. The Kilmoran family, Cathleen gathered, were desperately poor—when they weren't buying ten-guinea Siamese cats—living in a house that was ''falling to pieces for the want of a lick of paint,'' ruled over by the gorgon referred to as ''Herself;'' a curmudgeonly old great-aunt who was ''sitting on her money bags,'' as Mollie inelegantly phrased it. ''If Randy had a free hand—as he will have when he inherits the estate—he says he would spend every penny of the idle capital to stock the sort of a farm that would make a fortune for us in no time. With the whole world short of meat, he says . . . .''

But what Randy Kilmoran had said about the world food shortage was lost in hideous confusion as the front wheels of the car went over an enormous boulder that Mollie had been too busy chattering to see in time. Disentangling Mr. Yo-Yo's frenziedly clutching paws from her hair, Cathleen peered hopefully at the massive stone gateway through which they were swerving, but if this were the driveway to the Kilmoran house it wasn't much better than the stony lanes. Bounding miraculously from pothole to pothole, the car drew up at last at the foot of a flight of weed-grown steps. There was an open door, revealing a vast, stone-paved hall, dimly lit and hung with the glassy-eyed heads of very defunct stags. Extricating herself from the car, more dead than alive, Cathleen followed Mollie Kilmoran into this cavernous entry, her weary spirit quailing at the sight of the tall, forbidding old lady who came forward to meet them, a lorgnette lifted to her eyes in haughty inquiry.

"You have brought someone to visit us, Mollie?" this apparition demanded in the thin, remote voice of old age.

"It's Miss Trenton, grandam," Mollie announced, with a breeziness that couldn't quite conceal the nervous tremor in her tone. "A great friend of Randy's . . . she traveled over from London with him last night. . . ."

"Indeed!" The lorgnette flashed into action once more as Cathleen put out an uncertain hand.

"My great-aunt, Lady FitzOsborne," she heard Mollie murmur in introduction, and it was as though the very stones of the ancient floor turned to water beneath her feet. Dimly she was aware of the fingers that touched her own, light and brittle—and dry as bloodless bone. And beyond the roaring in her ears she could hear the old voice, thin as a whisper from the grave.

"Welcome to Castle Osborne," Lady FitzOsborne said.

CHAPTER TWO

JUST FOR A MOMENT, then, it was all so exactly like a terrible dream that afterward Cathleen could never be quite sure if it was only her own sense of horror that filled the hall, or if the tall gaunt woman facing her did actually sway a little, her eyes fixed and glittering, her fleshless lips sagging. Nor could she be sure that the shaking throat did utter the sounds that might have been that trembling question, "Why have you come here?"

Then the horrible stillness broke up abruptly like splintered glass, as Randy Kilmoran strode in followed by a scurry of large noisy dogs. With a yell of defiance the Siamese kitten leaped from Mollie's arms to the antlers of the nearest dead stag, the dogs in hot pursuit, their excited barking and the howlings and spittings of Yo-Yo filling the place with a pandemonium so overwhelming that it acted like an anaesthetic, numbing all feeling.

Vaguely Cathleen was aware of a great many things happening at once. The hall seemed to be suddenly filled with people—and activity. Randy hitting out at the dogs, Mollie climbing on an oak chest to rescue Yo-Yo, calling frantically, "Lanty Conor! Lanty, where are you? Come and take these beastly dogs back to the stables!" The young man who was apparently Lanty came running in, followed by an elderly woman with a peasant red handkerchief tied over her gray hair, her hands lifted in protest as she cried out, "Wirrah! Wirrah, Miss Mollie, have ye no care for herself with yer noise and foolishness!" And there was Lady FitzOsborne swooning dramatically into a vast crimson velvet armchair, her white head lolling like a broken flower.

Abandoning dogs and cat, Mollie rushed to her side, while Randy and the peasant woman stooped over her. Stranded and alien in the midst of the cold, wide flagstones, Cathleen stood stricken, her heart beating violently, her thoughts chaotic. She was aware, even at that tumultuous instant, of the bold, pale eyes with which Lanty surveyed her; a boy with the blond beauty of a Viking warrior, wearing the green baize apron of a household servant. Driving the dogs before him he turned to give her a last coldly inquisitive stare before the dark opening of some domestic passageway swallowed him up.

Tottering forward on legs that did not seem to belong to her, Cathleen joined the group around the crimson chair. "I must not stay here! I cannot stay!" she heard herself murmur in lost despair, and it was Randy who turned to her, laying a reassuring hand upon her shoulder.

Afterward she was to remember the real kindliness in the gray eyes looking down at her, but for the moment no kindliness, no reassurance could reach her.

"I have killed her!" she whispered.

And it seemed to her the most heartless thing in the world that Randy could laugh, saying, "You poor kid; what a welcome for you! For heaven's sake don't look so scared. Lady FitzOsborne has these heart attacks every time she leaves her room—she has no business to be wandering around the house this hour of the night."

"Look!" he said. Then, as one might speak to a frightened child, "You sit there on that bench while I carry herself upstairs. Sit there and talk to the little cat."

She felt herself pushed gently onto a settle of night black bog oak, and with a comprehensive gesture Randy picked up Yo-Yo and placed him on her lap. Holding the small, quivering animal, Cathleen saw the unreal scene play itself out; Randy lifting the fragile old lady in his arms and carrying her up the cavernous stairs, the muttering peasant woman following. Then Mollie, brushing the hair out of her eyes with an exhausted air, came young and thin toward her, her pointed pixie face quite calm, her green eyes smiling.

"You'll be dying of hunger," she said apologetically. "And my poor little Yo-Yo, too." She took the cat eagerly in her arms, rubbing her cheek on the brown, velvety head. "Let's go and see what we can rustle up to eat. Randy has already eaten, I expect." Just as though swooning dowagers mattered not at all!

"Lady FitzOsborne!" Cathleen brought out jerkily. "I . . . cannot stay here. She is ill." And through the mists of horror that enfolded her she wanted to cry out . . . . *Because I am a face from her own, her cruel past—a dead hand laid on her heart. She recognized me. I know she did!*

But the words did not come, nor could she have spoken them to save her life. The drama must go on now as it had commenced, in awful silence. Too much had happened too quickly and there was no way of knowing what she ought to do—only that she longed to escape, to wake and find the whole ghastly business no more than some trick of uneasy sleep.

Following the lightly chattering Mollie she found herself in a vast and lofty room, the walls paneled in dark gleaming wood, the tall mullioned windows uncurtained. Two oil lamps made pools of light on a long oval table of exquisite design—Chippendale perhaps, Cathleen thought vaguely, seeing the strange medley of dishes and food strewn before her—a silver epergne, piled with exotic peaches and grapes, flanked by a tray bearing a brown kitchen teapot and a loaf of roughly cut bread. There was an immense cold ham, an oven-stained casserole piled with potatoes cooked in their jackets, plates of butter in extravagant, inelegant lumps and a beautiful decanter filled with ruby wine.

"It's only the cheapest of Algerian, but it's better than stewed tea," Mollie was saying, pouring the wine into glasses that looked as though they ought to be in a showcase in a museum. "Drink some, please, Miss Trenton, you look absolutely ghastly!"

Automatically Cathleen raised the goblet to her lips.

"It has upset you seeing herself collapse," Mollie rattled on. "You're very sensitive, aren't you? Or perhaps it is that we aren't sensitive enough. We've got so used to grandam's heart attacks; even used to the thought that sooner or later one of those attacks may prove fatal. Do I sound heartless?" Mollie gave a small shrug. "It isn't as though she were a very lovable person, you know . . . and she is only the remotest kind of relative."

"But you live with her?" Cathleen said in a tone so sharp with curiosity that instantly she was ashamed of it. "I mean . . . this *is* your home, isn't it?" she added more gently.

"Only since after the war, when Randy came out of the Navy and Lady FitzOsborne decided to make him her heir. I think as far back as that the doctors had told her her heart was failing and she wanted to set her affairs in order. It was all something of a surprise to us, because we're really quite a distant branch of the family. Our grandfather was Lady FitzOsborne's second cousin . . . or even third, perhaps. . . ." Mollie's voice trailed away abstractedly as she scooped Yo-Yo out of the ham dish. "He's starving, poor lamb! What do I give him? I'm sure this fat, boiled ham is too rich for him. The breeder we bought him from has sent me a diet sheet I haven't yet had time to read properly; but it seems he ought to have things like scraped raw meat and steamed fish. . . ."

Wriggling from her grasp, the kitten made a playful dash at the shining epergne and watched in rapt delight as a dislodged peach rolled slowly across the polished table. Raising himself then to pounce, he stood on his hind legs, poised and motionless as a ballet dancer, his slim brown paws clasped quaintly across his heart.

"Isn't he adorable!" Mollie sighed in ecstasy. "Randy will

kill me if I don't train him to keep off the table. But just for tonight I can spoil him.'' She poured cream into a saucer and Yo-Yo flung himself upon it with wolflike greed.

''Wasn't there any nearer relative than your brother for Lady FitzOsborne's heir?'' Cathleen asked, no longer caring whether she sounded impertinently inquisitive or not. There was so much now that she had to know. This shadowy room with the half-seen portraits glimmering on its walls seemed to throb with unseen presences. Her mother . . . had she really sat at this self-same table, drunk from these antique glasses, touched with her young, thin hands that heavy silver dish with a load of fruit ripened by some long-dead summer? If only Mollie could be induced to speak of these things! With a shiver of suppressed excitement Cathleen looked at the small, artless face bent above the lapping Yo-Yo. ''Had Lady FitzOsborne no child of her own?'' she asked in a thread of a voice.

''There *was* a daughter,'' came the answer, as still distracted by the kitten, Mollie sliced ham onto a plate and piled potatoes beside it. ''Have some food,'' she offered, pushing the plate across the table.

''A daughter?'' echoed Cathleen, in desperation. With a sigh Mollie seemed to pull her thoughts away from her new pet. ''It's quite a story,'' she said. And then, because she was too young to be discreet, and because the story she had to tell echoed with the drama all youth enjoys, she went on freely to say that Lady FitzOsborne's only child had been born to her parents late in their lives. ''They'd made up their minds it was to be a son—to carry on the name. Probably,'' said Mollie with the precociousness of the modern young, ''they only decided to have it at all because they wanted a boy. And when it turned out to be a girl they hated it.''

''Oh!'' cried Cathleen, in a small wounded voice. ''How awful!''

''Yes, wasn't it?'' Mollie agreed lightly. ''The girl's name was Sheila and she must have been dreadfully lonely growing up in this great house ignored by her mother—her father died quite soon after her birth—and with no companions of her own age. A Kilmoran aunt of ours who used to visit here has told me about those days and how poor little Sheila ran wild with the peasant children around about. Until all of a sudden her mother—that's grandam, of course—realized she was growing up and decided to marry her to a Kilmoran so that the property could be taken over and run by a male who was at least a relative. She chose an uncle of ours—twice Sheila's age. She was eighteen then and she must have been terrified when this middle-aged Kilmoran turned up to claim her. Anyway, she'd been busy falling in love on her own account . . . with the grandson of that old woman in the red handkerchief you saw just now. Her name is Mary Costello and she has been grandam's personal maid ever since they were both seventeen . . . she adores grandam. But the thing about her grandson, Michael, is that he was devastatingly good-looking . . . like Lanty Conor. Lanty is a Costello, too, you see, on his mother's side . . . .''

''Oh!'' moaned Cathleen once more in inarticulate grief, her heart dying within her, her thoughts drowning in pity and confusion. Her mother . . . that dream figure, half girl, half woman, pressing so close through the shadows she seemed to come—not in one, but in many forms—a lost and lonely child, a frightened girl, a woman weeping in the arms of so wild a lover—like Lanty, a man with golden hair and the cold pale eyes of a Nordic god.

''He was terrific with horses,'' Mollie was recounting between mouthfuls of ham. ''Trained racers for Lord Dunlargan, who used to live in a great estate the other side of the lough. He came here to teach Sheila riding—'' She broke off. ''But doesn't all this bore you frightfully?''

''Oh no, no.'' Cathleen murmured passionately and, seeing the mild wonder in Mollie's green eyes, added hastily, ''It's so different to anything one could possibly hear in Petunia Road, where I live . . . I mean.'' She ended lamely, ''It's like something out of a book, isn't it?''

Mollie nodded. ''And it gets more and more melodramatic as it goes on. It was Mary who discovered the romance, you see, and instead of being honored that Miss Sheila had taken a fancy to her grandson she was furious—because, of course, of the difference in religion. The FitzOsbornes are Protestants. Anyway old Mary went up in the air good and proper—rushed to Lady Fitz with the whole story and there was a first-class row. Poor Sheila was actually locked up in the Tower Room. I'll show it to you tomorrow, it's a most horrible place. . . .''

Cathleen shielded her eyes with one shaking hand—a small defensive gesture as though she sought to shut out something too painful to be looked upon. And there would be no tomorrow, she resolved, for she could not remain in this house in which her mother had been so cruelly wronged. How right her father had been when he had told her in bitterness that there could be no happiness for her in any contact with the strange, warped creature who was Lady FitzOsborne! The thought of having to see her again even for a moment in the briefest of casual encounters made Cathleen feel as though she were suffocating. She would leave Castle Osborne first thing in the morning, she resolved . . . even if it meant the end of a holiday from which all zest had gone. She would go back to the empty house in Petunia Road, join the family in Bognor and endure the dreary attentions of Len Cranston; anything rather than remain in this atmosphere tainted with old cruelties, old hates.

''It was on the very night before her wedding to the middle-aged Kilmoran that Sheila ran away,'' Mollie's fresh young voice was rippling on. ''Mike Costello was waiting for her with a boat and he rowed her across the lough to a distant parish where there was a milk train leaving for Dublin. It seems they were married in Dublin, and Lady Fitz disowned her daughter from that day—was never heard to speak her name again. It was as though she had never existed. Nobody seems to know or care what became of her after that. But I think if she had ever tried to come home there would have been murder,'' Mollie ended, with simple relish.

With a shiver Cathleen remembered the old malignant eyes peering at her through a shaking lorgnette . . . in what might have been dawning recognition. And looking up she saw Randy Kilmoran come into the room, an immense and shadowy form crossing the dark expanse of floor, until the pool of light from the table lamp revealed him more clearly. He looked tired—and taciturn, flinging one hand out in an impatient gesture to indicate in reproach the sly way Yo-Yo had insinuated himself between the potato casserole and the ham dish, so that he might crouch unseen to nibble the ham bone that stuck out over the end of the dish.

''Will you look at that cat!'' he exploded. ''Honestly, Mollie, you aren't fit to have the training of as much as a flea! What'll Miss Trenton think of us? Cats eating the food on the table . . . it might as well be pigs in the parlor and be done with it.''

Mollie giggled unrepentantly. ''To think of him crawling in behind the dish where I couldn't see him!'' she exulted. ''He's got brains, so he has! The first time he ate the ham openly and I scolded him . . . so he worked it out in his little mind—''

''For heaven's sake stop blathering and take that unfortunate starved animal down to the kitchen and get him a suitable meal,'' Randy ordered in a roar that brooked no contradiction. Mollie picked up the kitten and slid tactfully away.

In the momentary silence that followed her departure, Cathleen fingered the stem of her wineglass and, glancing covertly at the man sitting opposite her, thought how odd it was that he should be a relative—a man upon whom she had stumbled in the accidental proximity of a railway journey, her cousin . . . her kinsman! What on earth would he say if she were to tell him so? But she had no idea of complicating a fantastic situation still further by blurting out her identity. Pain . . . and something that was a strange and undefinable terror . . . sealed her lips. This muddle of family resurrection into which she had blundered could best be resolved by silence. She must get away as quickly as possible from all sight and sound of the woman of whom her father had said, "She doesn't know of your existence—and would have nothing to do with you if she did. . . " To speak out, then, would be but to invite humiliation. In this house that had spurned her mother, would not her mother's daughter also be spurned? And in loyalty to the dead she could wish it no other way.

Nevertheless, her heart ached strangely as she met the intent gray eyes levelly regarding her.

"Have some more of this red ink," Randy invited, hospitably holding out the carafe of wine.

Cathleen shook her head. "How is Lady FitzOsborne?" she inquired.

"Better," Randy returned easily. "She's had a dose of the sedative that her doctor ordered for these attacks, and she'll sleep now for hours I expect. Mary Costello will sit up with her tonight and no doubt she'll be more or less herself again in the morning."

"All the same, I don't feel I ought to stay," Cathleen was beginning nervously, when Mollie returned with Yo-Yo in one hand and a plate of flaked fish in the other.

"Of course you must stay," Randy interrupted rather impatiently. "I've already fixed it up with Mary Costello—who is our housekeeper. She's getting a bed ready for you right now You can't possibly go back to Callaghan's; they've no room for you."

"I can go home . . . back to London," Cathleen offered.

"Are we bad enough to drive you that far?" Randy asked reproachfully.

"No, of course not . . . it's not that in the least . . ." Cathleen floundered.

Randy stood up with a mighty yawn. "Sleep on it," he counseled. "Castle Osborne won't look so grim in the morning."

"You *can't* go off and disappoint us now, Miss Trenton," came the voice of Mollie from some shadowy outer region where she lay on the floor feeding the kitten. "Randy is counting on the money you are going to pay him to buy that four-pronged harrow he wants—aren't you, Randy?"

"Someday," said Randy, without heat, "I'm going to give myself the pleasure of tanning the hide off you, Miss Mollie Kilmoran. In the meantime, Miss Trenton will, I hope, take no notice of your impertinence." He smiled at Cathleen suddenly, disarmingly. "Castle Osborne," he said, "doesn't cater for *paying* guests . . . that's one thing herself was right about when she closed down on our unhappy experiment with boarders last summer. As long as you're stranded you're very welcome to stay here, and with the size of the house and the miles of the estate I can promise you we won't get in one another's way." The smile broadened into a mischievous grin. "Even if you *are* my great friend from London," he said softly, and there was a sound of smothered laughter from Mollie on the floor.

"I didn't know you heard me, Randy! I'm sorry, but I had to tell herself something that would account for Miss Trenton!"

Cathleen went crimson. "There's no need to account for me at all. I don't intend to stay . . . it's very kind of you to give me shelter for tonight . . . but after tonight—"

"Ah, come on now!" Randy put in good-humoredly, even coaxingly. "I'm surprised at you. Isn't it the most natural thing in the world that we should help Mrs. Callaghan out when she is packed to the doors, and here we are with maybe twenty empty bedrooms on our hands?"

There was no answering that. Somehow the sudden introduc-

tion of Mrs. Callaghan into the argument so completely floored
Cathleen that she could only stand there all but swaying visibly
in the access of sheer fatigue that all at once possessed her.
Everything was so hopelessly mixed up and she couldn't think
straight any longer. Only that she had the oddest desire to burst
into floods of bleak and bitter weeping . . . as though Randy
Kilmoran's remark about helping Mrs. Callaghan out had been
the most heartless affront, which, of course, was nonsense. It
was the long, tiring day that was making her want to weep—a
day that had been going on solidly for aeons of time—ever since
she'd left Petunia Road with her suitcase in her hand something
like thirty-nine hours ago. And then the arrival at Osbornestown
only to find herself unwanted; the far, far worse arrival at Castle
Osborne with all its dreadful revelations, and finally, of course,
that searing conversation with Mollie before Randy—who
really couldn't matter at all in all this—had come into the dining
room.

"I think I'd like to go to bed, please," Cathleen heard herself
say in a small, shaken voice.

CHAPTER THREE

IF SHE HAD IMAGINED that her longing to go to her room was simply a desire to be alone so that she might sort out her emotional turmoil, it didn't turn out that way at all. She was so tired that it seemed to her afterward she scarcely even saw her room that night—just the big four-poster bed with the sheets turned down invitingly, and old Mrs. Costello backing out of the door saying, ''Good night, now, miss, and I hope ye have all ye want; if not pull the bell handle there foreninst ye.'' And a moment or two later she had tumbled out of her clothes and into the bed and was fast asleep. Once or twice during the night she stirred in a drugged way, dimly aware of the odd noisiness of the corridor outside her room—people hurrying along the bare, uncarpeted boards, voices rising and falling, and below her window on the graveled drive endless cars seemed to come and go with much slamming of doors, as though some insane kind of party were going on. But she couldn't really waken herself to wonder about it, and when the dawn broke she fell into a sleep so deep that no sound could possibly reach her.

It must have been almost noon when she came to the surface slowly, like a deep-sea diver pushing up through shoals of warm, dark green water. Gradually the events and impressions of yesterday's tumult returned, robbed now that she was rested of their sharper terrors, so that she was able to look with quiet interest at the room in which she lay—great windows with threadbare tapestry curtains, ugly cumbersome Victorian furniture, an immense marble-topped washstand bearing a toilet set of black china sprinkled with violent magenta roses. On the vast and chilly floor there were tattered rugs to hide the cracked linoleum; faded texts hung upon the damp-stained walls, and one huge oleograph depicting a mournful female clad in a voluminous nightgown clinging to a cross in the midst of a raging sea—a tasteless, uncared for room, mustiness pervading it like the very breath of desolation.

Turning to the windows Cathleen saw that the sun was shining and, jumping out of bed, she ran barefoot over the cold oilcloth to look out on such vistas of wild loveliness that a soft cry came to her lips. Arriving in Osbornestown in the dusk last night there had been no sign of the famous lough; so that now with dramatic unexpectedness it lay before her, miles and miles of milk-blue water studded with small verdant islands. Mountains on every side melted soft as chiffon into a heat-hazed sky. In the foreground the lands of Castle Osborne rolled in green terraces down to a sandy bay, fringed by young larch trees and just beneath the bedroom windows a pleasure garden that at some time or other had been laid out with formal care, rioted now in weed-grown disorder. Roses, lavender, hydrangeas, bearing outsize blooms of pale pink and softest blues flung tides of color between the overgrown box hedges. A broken stone cupid, like love overthrown, lay on his face beside a lily pond. The scent of the roses rising in the moist air, the scent, too, of sun-hot pines and rich, rank grasses, filled Cathleen with a strange excitement. That lush, earthy sweetness that is the very breath of the enchanted lands of Connemara—encountering it for the first time emotion stirred her heart, as though old dreams awakened.

As she dressed hurriedly, washing in the peat-brown water from the hideous black ewer, she had the oddest feeling of being not quite herself; possessed a little, her identity, its outlines blurred, submerged in the shadowy, undefinable feeling of some other haunting personality. It was as though she were partly that earlier replica of herself . . . her own mother. And it was with the sense of the eighteen-year-old Sheila urgent in her blood, rather than in her thoughts, she went downstairs; so lost in her bewitched mood that she did not notice the deserted air of the great house, nor its utter quietness.

Passing through the stone-paved hall with its grim antlered heads, she went out into the shining, beckoning day, running through the wild flower garden to the beaten path that led through the green fire of larches to the lake's edge. How still the water was—like lightly breathing silk, and soft as silk to the touch when she stooped to dabble her hands in it. She would swim here in this sheltered cove, she thought, and remembered with a pang how she had sworn to herself last night that she would go away. Turning then, she saw the bulk of the great house with its limestone turrets, moss-grown and crumbling as though they belonged to a much older time than the neat Victorian Gothic wings that had been built onto them. Hunger stirred in her heart—a longing to know the history of every stone of this place from which she must—like Sheila—be forever outcast.

Hearing the sound of oars grinding on oarlocks, she looked back to the lough again and saw a boat approaching—rowed by a man with bright gold hair. Lanty Conor, the good-looking houseman. What was he doing out on the lough at this hour of the day? Perhaps he had taken the Kilmorans over to one of the islands for fishing or swimming. As he pulled into the shore his glance for her was glowering and sullen and, tying the boat to a casual boulder, he would have passed her without greeting if she had not spoken. What time did the bus leave Osbornestown for Dunbarragh, she found herself inquiring—almost against her will; for it was as though the beauty all around her held her now in its bright enchantment—her own country, her lost and lovely birthright!

"It goes at eight in the morning, miss—the only bus of the day," Lanty was saying.

So she had missed any chance there might have been of slipping away from Castle Osborne without any fuss or explanation. Unless she asked Mollie to use precious gas in taking her the twenty miles to the nearest railway station, she must wait now until tomorrow.

With something like a feeling of reprieve she made her way back to the house, conscious of a longing for the breakfast it was probably much too late to hope for. Entering the stone-flagged hall she stood hesitant, noticing now the desolate stillness of the place and its uncared for air; the ashes of last night's fire unswept in the great hearth, Randy's gunnysack on the floor by the door where he had flung it down, the little white shawl that had slipped from the shoulders of Lady FitzOsborne when she collapsed still lying by the crimson chair where it had fallen. Where was everyone—the servants . . . the young Kilmorans? She thought of Lanty rowing around the lake when surely he would have been much better employed in the domestic tasks that so obviously awaited him. But perhaps Irish households are like that . . . timeless, haphazard.

Looking around in a lost way, wondering what to do with herself next, she saw the massive door leading from the hall and remembered it opened to the dining room. Hunger once more assailed her as she turned the handle of the door, and there before her was the long, beautiful table—still littered with last night's ham and old brown teapot and half-eaten loaf. Only that, like the Mad Hatter's Tea Party in *Alice*, all these viands had been pushed aside to make room for the dishes of a later meal, over which sat Randy, Mollie and an odd-looking man in a whitish raincoat.

Slowly the three heads turned as Cathleen entered, feeling more and more like an intruder every moment as she murmured her apology for having slept so late. There was something alarming about the blank look Randy gave her—almost as though he did not recognize her—and Mollie's murmured,

"Good Lord, Miss Trenton! I'd forgotten all about you!" did nothing to help.

Randy stood up then, saying with obvious effort, "Good morning, Miss Trenton. I hope you weren't disturbed last night by all the comings and goings?" Something somber in the tone halted Cathleen's heart.

"I did hear voices now and then," she faltered, "and cars . . . did anything . . . happen, then? Lady FitzOsborne?" she ended in a small, scared whisper, and knew even before Randy spoke again what she was going to hear. Lady FitzOsborne had died at four o'clock, just as the new day was dawning. "Soon after you went up to your room she had another seizure," Randy was explaining. "I went for the doctor. He did all he could . . . was with her until the end. . . ."

"God rest her!" sighed the man in the raincoat, raising a glass of what looked like whiskey to his lips, as though he drank some macabre toast to the shade of the departed lady.

"Mr. Philligan, our family solicitor," Randy indicated, with a nod in the raincoat's direction. "This is Miss Trenton, Phil, a young lady who is staying with us."

Mr. Philligan rose and bowed. "A sad visit, Miss Trenton, but, indeed, it will be company for Miss Mollie here to have you along with her in the tragic days that lie ahead."

Weakly Cathleen sank into the chair by Mollie's side . . . seeing now how tired and disheveled the child looked, as though she had spent the night in her clothes.

Mr. Philligan, having finished his whiskey in one appreciative gulp, seemed to be preparing to leave them. "Well, there's nothing more we can do for the moment," he was saying. "Only to keep on searching. . . ."

"There's nowhere to search," Randy insisted, in a weary voice. "I tell you it was always in the safe she kept it. . . ."

"A safe she never locked because she couldn't be bothered to remember the combination!" Mr. Philligan put in with a shrug.

"It was there a week ago," Randy said.

"And within the space of that week?" said Mr. Philligan, assuming all at once an excessively shrewd and legal manner. "Tell me now, was there any circumstance during that time that could . . . conceivably . . . have caused Lady FitzOsborne to change her mind about the disposal of her estate?"

"The only thing out of the way that happened," said Randy, was that I went to an Agricultural Show in London and came home again . . . and that Miss Trenton here arrived."

"Ah!" Mr. Philligan murmured, with fatuous significance. "You went to London. Tell me now. . . ." But what he wanted to be told faded into an incoherent murmur as the two men left the room.

"It's Lady FitzOsborne's will," Mollie explained wanly, as she poured coffee for Cathleen. "It's absolutely extraordinary—but it has simply disappeared. We went to look for it when Mr. Philligan came this morning, because it contained all the instructions grandam left about her funeral . . . and it has . . . just vanished." She yawned behind a small, grubby hand, a tired child with tousled red gold hair and frightened eyes.

"I'm so sorry!" Cathleen offered gently. "About everything . . . your sudden bereavement. . . ."

"It's . . . awe inspiring," Mollie whispered. "Death I mean. I've never seen anyone die before. But . . . I didn't really love grandam; it's no use pretending about it now, because last night was so awful and because I'm scared of . . . well, funerals and things." She turned and put out an impulsive hand. "Please don't go away, Miss Trenton . . . please stay here a little while with us . . . at least until the funeral is over!"

Cathleen put a quick arm around the thin, childish shoulders, "Of course I'll stay if I can be of any help . . . if you won't feel that I'm intruding?"

"Oh, no, you won't be intruding. It will be wonderful to have you . . . give us something else to think about besides this awful worry over the will. You see, if it really *is* lost, or if in some moment of madness herself *did* destroy it, it means Randy won't inherit Castle Osborne after all . . . and I think that would kill him. This place means so much to him. He has such marvelous plans for developing the land. But unless we find the will Mr. Philligan says it will have to go to the next of kin. That means they'll have to search for the lost Sheila, the daughter I was telling you about yesterday.''

Cathleen went ashy white. ''And if she happened to be dead?'' she asked, in a thread of a voice.

''Then Mr. Philligan says it would go to her children—if she had any. In any case, Castle Osborne probably will be lost to Randy.'' And even as she spoke there sounded through the quiet house a dreadful rising wail of grief—more elemental than human. Bleak as the snow winds over winter wastes the strange sound swelled and died. In frozen immobility Cathleen listened, her blue eyes darkening as the pupils distended.

''It's Mary Costello keening,'' Mollie whispered, ''Poor Mary! She loved my great-aunt.''

CHAPTER FOUR

THAT BLOOD-CURDLING cry of grief, Cathleen was to hear it many times in the somber week that followed, and as long as she lived she would remember the funeral with its background of almost feudal ceremony. It was all so strange, so far removed from Petunia Road!

Day after day in the darkened hall the coffin stood on a high purple-draped bier. White flowers, white candles with their living petals of golden flame filled the air with odors of rose and lily and melting wax. Endlessly there sounded the hushed footfalls of the constant stream of visitors, the murmur of voices muted in prayer as men in homespun and women in shawls dropped on their knees by the coffin's side. The Lady of Castle Osborne was dead, and from every neighboring village the simple people came to pay their last respects.

There were other visitors, less simple; tweed-clad, hearty souls who arrived in battered cars that had traveled the width of Ireland. The ragged remnants of the vanishing "gentry" of Anglo-Irish days. In the dining room—in which the Mad Hatter's Tea Party atmosphere increased hourly—they were entertained to cold chicken and ham lunches, strong tea and potent whiskey drunk neat from the exquisite Waterford-glass goblets. While in the kitchen the peasant people sat day and night smoking their short clay pipes, reciting like characters from the chorus of a Greek tragedy the virtues and graces of the departed.

Each day tradesmen's vans came the twenty miles from the

shops of Dunbarragh bringing fresh cases of whiskey and casks of porter, great slabs of bright yellow grocery cake and the big dark loaves of sweet "barm brack" that kept the mourners going. It was like some grim topsy-turvy festival that would never end and in which all domestic order perished. There seemed to be no regular meal times; if one went to bed at nights it was only to be conscious that the great house continued to throb with a feverish undercurrent of wakefulness.

And through it all, like figures in a restless dream, Randy and Mr. Philligan—forever in his white raincoat—searched ceaselessly and hopelessly for the missing will. Sometimes Mollie and Cathleen were pressed into helping them. Tallboys, wardrobes, oaken chests filled with the miscellany of years accumulation, were turned inside out; Lady FitzOsborne's empty bedroom all but dismantled. Delving into dusty cupboards, peering into bureaux and bookcases, Cathleen moved in a daze of sheer disbelief. Here she was in Castle Osborne trying to find a will that affected her whole future. For if it was not found the fact of its nonexistence made her the heir to this vast, if poverty-stricken, estate. It couldn't be really happening to her! It wasn't true! Presently she would wake up in Petunia Road and hear her stepmother telling her it was time to get up and rush off to the office!

Time and again she would push the cluster of dark curls back from her brow in a gesture of weariness, trying to clear her brain and sort out her confused, unhappy thoughts. Ought she not to reveal herself at once to the Kilmorans, she would wonder. But, intimidated, she shrank from making an announcement that even to herself seemed madly incredible. *How can I prove I am Sheila FitzOsborne's daughter*, she would ask herself helplessly. Supposing they didn't believe her—or, worse still, thought she had somehow contrived to smuggle herself into the castle at this juncture incognito in order to spy out the land. Looking back on the sequence of events that had brought her here it would not be a very reasonable suspicion. But panic-stricken people are not reasonable, and Randy and Mollie, it was clear, were very panic-stricken indeed; Randy tight-lipped and grim in his misery, Mollie, wide-eyed and voluble.

Shaking the mildewed leaves of the books in the dark old library the afternoon before the funeral, the two girls worked side by side, dusty, tired, possessed with the urgency of finishing this fatuous task upon which the fussy Philligan had insisted.

"As though grandam would have hidden her will in *here*!" Mollie grumbled. "There was no reason for her to hide it anywhere—nor did she hide it, I'm absolutely convinced. Only the day before Randy went to London she was talking to him about what he must do if she were to die before he came back—because she knew how uncertain her heart was and was quite brave about it. The will was in the safe then, a will leaving Randy *everything*. If it has disappeared someone has wilfully destroyed it."

"But who?" Cathleen faltered, thinking now in a fresh access of nervousness that the person who might most profitably destroy Lady FitzOsborne's will would be *herself*! Another good reason for keeping her mouth shut! Supposing, suggested Cathleen's tormented imagination, they decided she had crept into the castle for this reason and no other! A crazy idea—but no crazier really than the whole amazing and terrifying set of circumstances.

"Perhaps Lady FitzOsborne destroyed the will herself that last night . . . when she knew she was dying," Cathleen offered wildly.

"But why should she?"

Because she thought I was Sheila's ghost come back to reproach her, reflected Cathleen—even more wildly—and kept silent.

"It isn't," Mollie went on, "as if anything happened that

could have persuaded her to change her mind, and she wasn't a changeable person. She was set on Randy having the place; for the past two years she'd been grooming him for the responsibility that would come to him when she had gone. And it means *everything* to him.'' The green eyes filled with tears. ''You've no idea how awful it was for us when Randy came out of the navy, and we had nothing to live on. He went into a bank, a *bank*! Imagine Randy shut up day after day in one of those dreadful little cages full of other people's money! I think it would kill him to have to go back to that life. . . .''

''He mustn't go back to it,'' Cathleen heard herself declare, with curious passion. And just then the door of the library opened and Randy and Mr. Philligan came in.

''Any luck, ladies?'' inquired Mr. Philligan in his irritatingly breezy way.

''How *could* there be any luck,'' Mollie answered crossly. ''You know perfectly well it is sheer waste of time looking in these old books.''

''All the same,'' returned Mr. Philligan cheerily, ''we've got to leave no stone unturned. When anything of value is lost there is one simple rule to go by; look in all the likely places first . . . and if you draw a blank then look in all the unlikely places. . . .''

''If we're going to look in all the unlikely places in Castle Osborne,'' grumbled Randy, ''it will take us about a hundred years.''

With an unfeeling snigger Mr. Philligan threw himself into a saddleback armchair and took from his raincoat pocket an old and odorous pipe. ''Listen now, Randy, boy, and don't get disheartened. I'm doing all any man could do to help you. Didn't I sit up till all hours last night working out the whole family tree to its last ramifications . . . the FitzOsbornes of Connaught, the De Corsos of Mayo and the Kilmorans of Meath . . . not a one of them left that matters now excepting yourself and this missing Sheila who ran off with the Costello fellow. So that if we don't succeed in tracing her, or if she has died and left no issue, will or no will you'll be all right. You're the next of kin.''

"Is that a fact, Phil?'' Randy's voice was light with momentary relief.

"Of course it's a fact. Only we've got to prove that Sheila Costello is out of it . . . and that will take a certain amount of time and research. I've written explaining the whole situation to a Dublin firm of inquiry agents that does this kind of thing for us. . . .''

Unnoticed Cathleen crept out of the library at this point, her heart pounding, her blue eyes wild. In the privacy of her own room she stood before the tarnished mirror on the dressing table, her hands clenched, her breath coming unevenly. Randy sitting in the library downstairs, grim and lost—more vulnerable than she had dreamed he could ever be—hanging on to Mr. Philligan's words, as a drowning man clutches at a rope. Odd, how acutely it could hurt to see him like that! But if the Sheila complication could be kept out of the picture he might yet inherit Castle Osborne. All she had to do then was to keep silent. They would continue to search for Sheila a while; and in her ignorance, it seemed to Cathleen a hopeless enough quest. They didn't even know Sheila had married again . . . it was as Mrs. Costello they would seek to trace her. How, then, could they ever connect her with the Mrs. Trenton who had died so long ago in a London suburb? So that after a time the search would inevitably peter out and everything would be all right . . . for Randy.

Looking at herself in the mirror she saw her troubled eyes look back at her—uneasy eyes, frightened, questioning. Why all this concern for the feelings of Randy Kilmoran? Only that it was really concern for herself. She was afraid, horribly afraid of the fuss there would be if she were to go back to the library at this moment and tell Mr. Philligan and the Kilmorans who she really was. And still more frightened of what might happen afterward—assuming they believed her. She hadn't the remotest notion what proofs she might be required to furnish, nor what the legalities of such a situation might be. But supposing in the end she got Castle Osborne—the encumbered estate, the great shabby house. What on earth could she do with it all? The questioning eyes went blank, filming over with the sheer impossibility of peering into a future so utterly improbable. Once more the dreamlike feeling descended upon her, the daze of disbelief.

With a start she turned from the mirror at the sound of a cautiously opened door. It was old Mrs. Costello—halted on the threshold of the room, as though disconcerted to find it inhabited—her face under its peasant head shawl ravaged with weeping, the heavy eyes under their hooded lids sunken and glittering as if with fever.

"I thought you were below in the library, miss, and I bethought meself to come up and turn down the bed," the woman apologized sullenly, and somehow a little unconvincingly, for in all the days of mourning she had not once emerged from her gathering of wailing cronies in the kitchen to attend in any way to the comfort of the household, or of the guest.

In an odd, strained silence they looked at one another, the old woman and the young one. Something of snakelike intensity in the hooded eyes brought a flutter to Cathleen's overwrought nerves. Why did Mrs. Costello stare at her so strangely? Why had she come creeping up here in this sinister way . . . for obviously the bed was the flimsiest excuse.

"Did they find the will in the library?" the woman whispered.

Cathleen shook her head. *Mrs. Costello*, she was thinking . . . *that was the name my mother, too, once bore!* How strange, how terrifying it all was. Was it recognition once more

peering at her in those fathomless tear-stained eyes . . . even as it
had seemed to glitter from behind a lorgnette held in a trembling
hand a week ago? She said, speaking slowly, almost drowsily,
as though from the depths of the incomprehensible dream,
"How could they have found the will in the library when it was
forever kept in the safe in Lady FitzOsborne's room? It is just
that Mr. Philligan has to satisfy himself that we have looked
everywhere."

"He has his duty to do," the old woman agreed with a sigh.
"But it will be a long duty I'm thinking, and may well take us all
to the courts of law before it is at an end."

"Unless they find Lady FitzOsborne's daughter," Cathleen
forced herself to say, obeying now the urge taking shape in her
mind, bracing her courage. There were questions she had
vaguely known she must ask of this woman . . . and here was her
opportunity.

"Did Lady FitzOsborne speak to you of her daughter that
night after she was taken ill, Mrs. Costello?" she asked.

A flicker of something that might have been resentment lit the
withered face. "Why should she speak on that night a name that
for twenty-two years never once crossed her lips?"

"Because . . . she was dying," Cathleen offered tremulous-
ly. "Sometimes at the last . . . people change. I know I am a
stranger in this house . . . that it is not my business; only that I
am anxious to help Mr. Kilmoran and his sister. And it did occur
to me to wonder if Lady FitzOsborne herself could possibly
have had anything to do with the disappearance of her will?"

Mrs. Costello laughed, briefly, unpleasantly. "Your concern
for the Kilmorans does you credit, miss," she sneered—for
there was no mistaking the scorn in her voice. "If it is any ease
to you to know it, let me assure you that Lady FitzOsborne—
living or dying—would *never* change. That night . . . from the
moment she fell down in her weakness below in the hall there
was no word out of her, nor could she have found the power to

move her will from the safe even if she had wanted to, for she never regained full consciousness. She died, I believe, as she lived, disowning the child who wronged her. . . .''

''Was the wrong so grievous?'' Cathleen whispered.

''Ingratitude . . . willfulness. . . .''

''Love,'' Cathleen put in softly.

Mrs. Costello shrugged. ''A love that wrecked three lives—her own, her mother's and the man at whom she flung herself that black and hapless night she left her home. My grandson knew well it meant ruin for him when he took her away across the lough—but she gave him no choice. . . .''

''She was eighteen,'' Cathleen offered pitifully.

''And our Mike but two years more—a lad with his future bright before him until she forced him into marriage out of his class, out of his faith.'' She broke off, her hooded eyes watchful now and curiously alight. ''You are interested in the story of our old sorrows?'' She whispered with strange and sinister emphasis.

Cathleen colored under that wary glance. ''It is simply that Mollie has been talking to me of these things . . . because of the lost will. . . .''

''Miss Mollie has the tongue of a babbling child,'' Mrs. Costello said disapprovingly. With a curious flick of her hands then, a gesture of dismissal or disgust, the woman turned away. ''I'll do the bed some other time,'' she mumbled and was gone, leaving Cathleen with a sense of uneasiness difficult to define.

But she was becoming hopelessly nervy, she told herself. There had been nothing personal in Mrs. Costello's strange manners and seeming innuendoes. How could there have been? And at least she was assured now that there had been no fantastic developments on Lady FitzOsborne's deathbed. In the back of her mind there had lingered all along that uncomfortable suspicion of having been recognized. But whatever the basilisk eyes behind the lorgnette had seen—they had kept their secret.

So that, Cathleen comforted herself, there need be no qualms of conscience on *that* score. The loss of the will had been the veriest accident. Lady FitzOsborne had died believing that Randy Kilmoran would be her heir . . . *wanting* it that way. Wasn't it only just then that her wishes should be respected? Even stony-hearted unforgiveness assumes a certain sanctity from the other side of the grave!

Or at least that was what Cathleen was persuading herself as she went downstairs, finding yet another good reason for her evasive silence. Though what could she do but be silent? A case for the courts, Mrs. Costello had summed it up—the awful, bitter wrangle of a disputed will. Oh no, it must never come to that . . . she couldn't bear it, Cathleen thought with a shiver. Her own claims being asserted before some hard-eyed judge . . . Randy Kilmoran's counter claims, the dwindling capital dwindling still further under the inroads of a long legal procedure. Much to better slip away, go back to Petunia Road where the bungling Mr. Philligan wouldn't in a hundred years catch up with her. Tomorrow when the funeral was over she would go away . . . forget the whole fantastic affair as though it were the queer dream it truly seemed.

Slipping out of the house she made her way to the overgrown flower garden where the neglected roses dropped their petals in sweet confusion on the poor little fallen cupid. Tears pricked at her eyes . . . stupidly, unaccountably, for why should she weep because flowers died untended and lake waters dreamed and mountains were lifted in distant loveliness to a pearly evening sky? Like a hand laid in quietness on her feverishly planning heart the tranquil scene seemed at once a comfort and a reproach. Petunia Road . . . how alien and unreal the thought of her English home seemed all at once! How could she leave all this beauty and mystery to return to the drab suburban round that was her life?

Hurrying through the garden, as though it held for her now

some intolerable quality, she came to a gate that led into an overgrown lane hedged in by blackberry bushes, the long grass starred with meadowsweet and velvety foxgloves. In her brief excursions away from the house it was always toward the lake she had drifted, but this evening unseeingly, mindlessly she walked for the mere sake of walking, not caring where her feet took her. And presently she found her way barred by a high stone wall in which a wicket gate swung half-open. Pushing her way through the aperture she saw before her a vast kitchen garden in which apple trees, fruit bushes, giant rhubarb plants grew in junglelike profusion. Here unlike the flower garden, however, the box borders had been trimmed a little, the paths roughly weeded and there were patches of relative order in which cabbages and lettuces and potatoes appeared in neat rows. Shut in on all sides by the twenty-foot limestone wall, the sheltered ground, still holding the heat of the day's sun, gave out a rich perfume of moist soil and ripening fruits in which the odor of strawberries predominated. Sniffing the air, Cathleen had the oddest feeling of familiarity—as though in some dream life she had been here before! So that she knew almost without looking that the turn of the path before her led to the greenhouses in which the unpruned grapevines rioted and the peaches ripened in rosy splendor. That slope beneath the apple trees—in the spring it would be a carpet of blue forget-me-nots, she thought, wondering dimly how she could know this. And all at once the strangest thing happened, for the forget-me-nots were there before her eyes, the apple trees foamed with pink and white blossom and a child in an old-fashioned sunbonnet and holland pinafore ran smiling with upstretched arms, reaching for the apple blossom under an April sky.

Brushing her hand across her eyes Cathleen stood arrested by this vision, feeling dizzy, not quite real, until the mirage or whatever it had been, faded. An outside attack of imagination, she told herself, moving forward, a little shaky about the knees.

Approaching the cluster of trees she saw that it was the small green apples of summer that weighted the old gnarled bows, and no child in a holland overall played there. It was Yo-Yo, the Siamese kitten, who rushed through the deep grass, a flurry of cream and fawn, his blue eyes vivid as the dream flowers might have been. With a hoarse, strange cry of greeting he leaped toward her, landing on the path at her feet with the odd ballet-dancing effect of his kind, holding the pose on tiptoe a moment, dramatically, self-consciously as though aware of his own grace and beauty.

Stooping to stroke the dark little head, she was aware of voices murmurous in the jungle of raspberry canes behind the apple grove, and there was Randy Kilmoran talking to an old gardener with bowed and fragile shoulders and a gentle, beautiful face. Like a saint, Cathleen thought, looking into that luminous, wrinkled countenance with a queer pang of love—the warmth so vivid, so immediate in her heart as though it had lain there ready and waiting for this moment.

"I was taking a little walk," she murmured a little awkwardly in answer to Randy's abstractedly inquiring glance. "I saw the gate of this garden open. . . ."

"Indeed then, miss, and you are very welcome!" It was the old gardener speaking, his smile, his graciousness making her free of this little domain that was his kingdom.

"It is a very beautiful garden," she said.

The old man shook his head. "No, but it is sad with the . . . wear and tear of the years . . . like myself. In the times that was, it was a very different place; when the trees were young and supple and I had four men under me forever trimming the weeds out of it, cutting the grass back, tending the fruits and the flowers in the hothouses. Not an evening went by in those days but I sent up to the big house the peaches and asparagus and fine young peas for her Ladyship's dinner table, the roses and carnations she would wear with her lacy gowns. Wasn't I only telling Mr. Randy about it just now; and the way poor little Miss Sheila would come here by the hour playing around me as I worked, a fine little girl in a pinafore and a sort of a big linen bonnet; the kind the quality do have to keep the sun from a child's fair skin. . . ."

"Telling me, too," sighed Randy, "of the fruit and vegetables that are going to waste for lack of the van that might take them into Dunbarragh to be sold to the hotels. A van I'll probably never be able to buy now. . . ."

"Herself, God rest her, would sell nothing," the old man said.

Somehow they were all drifting along together then, the old gardener garrulously droning on about other times, Randy not listening to him, pointing out to Cathleen the great beds of luscious strawberries rotting in the sun, the ruby and black currants dropping off the bushes, birds gorged with their plunder rising from the green boughs as they passed; Yo-Yo champing his small jaws at the sight of them in a frenzy of tigerish excitement.

A child in a pinafore and a big linen kind of a bonnet! Dazed and abstracted Cathleen lifted her dark-lashed eyes to Randy's face, not seeing him. "And all this going to waste for the lack of the organization herself would never agree to—the commercialism she was too proud to accept," he was saying. Suddenly the patient desolation of his tone pierced her preoccupation.

"And now that herself has gone?" she hinted gently.

"I am hamstrung by this infernal confusion about the will," he finished for her. "There was so much I had planned to do!"

She said a little breathlessly, "It will all come out right somehow. It *must* come right!"

They had reached another wicket gate now on the farther side of the garden and stepping across its high threshold, Randy looked back at her, over his shoulder. "If you would like to take your walk any farther I am going up Doon Hill to speak to the

cowman,'' he said, an invitation prompted, perhaps, by the
sympathy of her last remark. And yet as they climbed the
rock-strewn track that led upward into a wilderness of heather-
clad bog he did not speak of the unhappy events of the past few
days. Of the stony ground he talked, the impossibility of turning
it into anything but the roughest of grazing upon which only the
mountain sheep might thrive. ''Not that there isn't a lot of profit
in the same sheep,'' he said. ''Connemara mutton, there isn't a
more delicious meat in the world. If there was some way of
transporting it fresh and in marketable quantities to the famished
markets of Britain . . . .''

''Is this moorland . . . this hill we are climbing, all part of the
Osborne estate then?'' Cathleen inquired, with a pang of
excitement, a curious stirring of the blood.

''All this,'' he said, with a sweep of his hand, ''Doon Hill and
beyond to the borders of Cahirquillagh to the north. . . . As far as
you can see to the south where the lough forms a natural
boundary, and on the lough itself we own several of the
islands. . . .''

''We?'' Cathleen queried in a softly, throbbing tone.

''A slip of the tongue!'' Randy's laughter was hollow. ''I
have no part in it now,'' he added soberly. ''A wraith inherits
it. . . .''

A wraith! How apt the phrase he had chosen.

Halting in their climb they turned to look back at the lands
spread out beneath them, seeing the rock-strewn heights and
lush, rich valleys, the gray towers of Castle Osborne proud in its
setting of windblown trees. Stained by the evening light the
waters of the lough spread wide and faintly flushed between the
mountainous shores; the whole scene brushed by the soft bloom
of the magic western air, a world of blues and grays and rosy
olive glimpsed through a rainbow veil.

To possess this splendor of savage hills and dipping
meadows; to be a part of it . . . to feel that one *belonged*

here—the color mounted in Cathleen's cheeks and her breath came unevenly. And then in the silence that fell on them she became aware—too throbbingly aware—of the man at her side. A man in patched and shabby homespun, but standing in kingly arrogance, his feet in their rough farming boots planted astride the narrow path, his strong face dark and sorrowful as he looked, even as she had looked, on the lands waiting to be possessed. But by whom? Almost she could feel the question burning like acid in his soul.

He said suddenly, "You see that large field down there sloping to the lough?"

"The very green field?"

"Yes. A year ago it was a soggy morass of sedge and bog cotton. I drained it, ploughed it, planted it with clover. I was going to put a herd of Herefords in there . . . yearling bullocks and heifers. . . ." In his urgency he had placed a hand on her shoulder. "Pasture land rich enough to produce fat stock in a season," he said. She couldn't bear the controlled misery of his tone and, turning to him, her blue eyes were wet under their smoky lashes.

"Don't say it like that! As if it were all over. As if there were no more hope!" Her voice wasn't quite steady; the feel of his strong, hard fingers gripping her shoulder was doing the strangest thing to her heart. And looking down at her it was as if he were suddenly, and perhaps for the first time in their walk, wholly aware of her, a girl with ardent eyes and a soft, red quivering mouth. Slowly his hand dropped away from her as he gazed at her, studying the contours of the vivid, sensitive little face under its cloud of windblown hair.

"You with your Irish eyes," he said, musing and dispassionately, "how did you come from a place like Petunia Road, and what has England to do with you? Was it out of the Holyhead train I got you, or did the wild swans of Coole bring you on their wings over the loch water?

"Will you tell me what chance brought you here to us," he whispered, "this time of all times; to share in our trouble as if it was your own trouble; to stand by Mollie as a sister might have done and to listen to me now and my ravings about the will as though it mattered to you what is to become of me and my poor dreams? Sweet child . . . why do you care so much?"

The oddly poetic phrases spoken in cool detachment—as only an Irishman drunk with his own delight in rhetoric could speak them. Did he know what his words could do to her? And what would he say if she were to answer his final question . . . literally . . . truthfully; out of the blinding, unbearable revelation now flooding her senses? All her agonizing over the worries of Randy Kilmoran; oh, there was but the one poor foolish reason for it! She could see that now, achingly, bewilderedly while the gray eyes watched her in a tenderness that was yet so strongly objective and aloof.

"Your poor dreams," she echoed sadly. "Land . . . and cattle and fields to drain . . . is that all you have to wish for?"

"Isn't it enough?" he countered gently. "At all events those are the only kind of dreams I can afford, and at the moment even such husks of living as I ask are, it seems, to be denied to me."

They were climbing the hill once more then, reaching presently the white-washed cabin where the cowman lived. While Randy went into its peat-reeking darkness to talk to his employee, Cathleen rested on the low stone wall that enclosed the poor little holding. Watching the hens that picked hungrily at the bare stones of the cowman's yard, she sat in a dream waiting for Randy to return to her and knew even as her eyes absently surveyed the stack of turf built at the cabin's gable end and the donkey tethered to a ring by the door, that her life would never be quite the same again. So this was it, she thought in dazed acceptance—the flame and the glory and the suffering the poets all extol. She had fallen in love! With a man who hardly cared that she existed . . . and would hate her if he realized just what her existence might mean to him. The fates that juggle with human hearts . . . could they have played a trick more cruel, or one more potent with possibilities of endless pain?

CHAPTER FIVE

THE DAY after the funeral dawned windless and gray, the sky ruffled all over with feathers of high cloud; like a dove's breast, Cathleen thought. Dressing in the big, somber bedroom she saw, beyond the shabby window curtains, mountains and lough and rocky bogland vividly colored in the muted light; as though with the absence of the sun's glare they stood forth today unveiled. Details emerged sharply, the white cottages with their golden thatched roofs, the narrow, climbing roads, stone walls so loosely built that daylight shone through, giving a lacy, fragile effect that made them like no other walls in the world. So many walls everywhere! Mollie said it was because there were so many stones; every acre of land was covered with them. So that if you wanted to reclaim a field for cultivation the first thing you had to do was to build a wall . . . simply to get rid of the stones. There was Randy's beautiful green field down by the loch . . . with no cattle in it.

A rapt light in her eyes, Cathleen thought about . . . cattle! Forever now the name "Herefords" would be mixed up in her mind with the bittersweet rapture of that twilight evening walk down the long hill from the cowman's cottage. Randy had talked "Herefords" all the way home; the fine "doers" they were and the way the prices they fetched rose with every cattle fair in Dunbarragh. Because not only Britain, but the whole world was growing short of meat. But he had never been able to make Lady FitzOsborne see the connection between that world shortage and the money the coffers of Castle Osborne so sorely needed.

"Five or six hundred pounds she was going to spend this summer on roof repairs," Randy had said. "And she might as well have thrown the money away, for the old Castle roof needs more like two thousand spent on it to make any repairs effective. If she'd only realized that the five or six hundred spent on stock would bring a quick return of profit; that spending capital on things like roofs was just killing capital. . . ."

"But at least that five hundred pounds won't be wasted on roofs now," Cathleen had reminded him. And he had shrugged, fallen silent, as though remembering suddenly how pointless the whole conversation had become. Money that depended on the vagaries of a lost will; what was the use of talking about what might or might not be done with it?

And now looking out at the empty green field Cathleen was conscious of a strange sense of personal concern. Every day the fine grass and clover out there remained uneaten by fat little Hereford bulls was a day wasted. Figures Randy had quoted danced before her eyes.

Going downstairs to breakfast she tried to keep her mind on the excitement of figures—money that made money; because she wanted to avoid that other far more dangerous excitement that the prospect of entering the dining room roused in her. Randy would be there—big and casual, offering his gentle but detached good-morning. She had put on a blue linen dress today, the color of her eyes—tied her curls back with a thin fillet of scarlet ribbon. Vitality bubbled up inside her—urgent, uncontrollable, demanding an outlet. *I feel*, she thought crazily, *like a kettle on the point of boiling over—like a song waiting to be sung!*

Crossing the hall where the bier had so recently stood, she shivered in the ecstasy of her own remoteness from death. That grim old lady they had buried yesterday . . . had she ever felt this same wild tingling of life, this young and arrogant certainty that one would go on forever? Even being unhappy in this mood was

enthralling; the anguish of expectancy that halted the breath as a
hand was raised to open a door. And going into the immense,
darkly paneled dining room was, Cathleen felt, rather like
walking onto a stage to take her cue in a drama in which she
played her part. How important a part? And how would the
drama end? Perhaps it would end—quite simply and without
any drama at all—today. The Kilmorans had asked her to
remain with them until the funeral, and now the funeral was
over. Would they expect her to leave right away . . . and
wouldn't it be the wisest and safest thing to do? But lying awake
in the early dawn she had already asked herself these questions
and found no answer that was either wise or simple. All she had
found was her own heart's foolish turmoil and, with that turmoil
now quickening her pulses, she entered the dining room to find
Mollie and Randy seated at the long table—from which somebody had at last removed the debris of the funeral baked meats.
The whole room, indeed, had an air of having been roughly
cleaned . . . by Lanty Conor, perhaps, who, having been absent
from work for five solid days, appeared now bending over a
chafing dish on the vast sideboard.

He looked, Cathleen noted without much interest, both ill and
dirty, his linen house jacket woefully soiled, his golden hair
lank and dulled. And it was just as she slid into her chair amid a
murmur of general good-mornings that the manservant let out a
howl of pain, flung the chafing dish away from him with a lurid
oath, and rushed from the room.

There was a moment of shocked silence; then Mollie said in
kindly explanation of the outburst, "He must have burned his
fingers!"

Randy shrugged. "If he burned his entire hand off he has no
business to throw the bacon across the room and tear out
swearing. The fellow is drunk. He has been drunk the whole
week; in spite of the fact that I kept the kitchen supply of spirits
down to the minimum all through the days of mourning. It's

poteen, that's what it is. I've suspected for some time that he has secret sources of supply; probably brews the stuff himself on one of the islands.''

Cathleen remembered how she had seen Lanty coming in from the lake the first morning of her visit, and how obviously annoyed he had been at their encounter. She had thought nothing at the time of the loosely filled sack the man had carried, and wondered now if it contained bottles of this stuff Randy was talking about. ''Poteen?'' she murmured in a rather mystified tone.

''Illicit whiskey,'' Randy explained, ''distilled from potato. The lads in the wilds get a kick out of making it—mostly I imagine because it is illegal and there's all the thrill of hiding the stills from the police. But once a fellow gets a taste for the stuff he's no use to himself or anybody else: One of the first things I'd do if I had the running of this place would be to sack Mr. Lanty Conor!''

Because he was a drunkard . . . like his kinsman before him. Perhaps it ran in the family, Cathleen thought, with an inward shiver. Was it poteen that had started Michael Costello on the dissolute road that had led to his ultimely death? Her mother's first husband . . . a haunted look came into her blue eyes as the old tragic story stirred in her mind. A story that never seemed quite real no matter how often she returned to it. Her mother . . . and a man who looked like Lanty Conor, talked like Lanty Conor. . . . Absently surveying the upturned silver dish, the scatter of greasy bacon slices on the floor, she saw Yo-Yo, the kitten, emerge from some hidden lair to pounce on a rasher. As though it had been a mouse, he picked it up, worrying it, growling over it, while Mollie made for him with an exclamation of dismay. Evading her, the little cat raced across the room, the hair on his spine bristling with the excitement of being chased. Out through an open window he went with Mollie after him, and as the sound of her laughing expostulations faded into the distance silence settled on the room—a comfortable and friendly silence; like a calm and soothing river it flooded Cathleen's empty heart. Away from Randy—since the disturbing discovery of her feeling for him—the thought of him could loom challenging and terrifying. But confronted by his large casual person, his quizzical gray eyes, and absentminded charm of manner she was instantly at rest. Just to be watching him now across this littered breakfast table, seeing him flick over the heap of mail beside his plate made her feel safe and content.

"All these bills," he was saying presently, with that careless Kilmoran candor that seemed to scorn all family reticence. "The creditors are flocking like vultures—and addressing the accounts to me. It was an open secret around the county that I was to step into the old lady's shoes."

"You mean you have to pay all these debts?" Cathleen asked, once more aware of that sharp tug of personal concern.

"Not for the moment. The person really responsible is, I suppose, the inheritor of the estate . . . or simply the estate itself. But until things are straightened out nobody gets a penny. Everything has to wait until the will—or absence of a will—is proved."

"And in the meantime," asked Cathleen, with a sudden uncomfortable awareness of the practical implications of the situation, "what happens about day-to-day expenses . . . servants' wages, and so on?"

"We just drift along. The bank will give me a certain amount of credit, I daresay. But it is all very awkward. Philligan is going up to Dublin today to see if he can hurry things on a bit."

"They haven't found any trace of Lady FitzOsborne's daughter then?" Cathleen put in a little breathlessly.

"Nothing fresh . . . only what we all knew already; that Costello was killed in a steeplechase soon after Sheila married him; after that she seems to have vanished into thin air."

Cathleen drew in a long, careful breath. So it was all working out just as she had foreseen. The thought brought no expected surge of relief, but the wildest impulse instead to lean across the breakfast table and say, ''I can tell you what happened to Sheila FitzOsborne, if you really want to know!'' Color fluttered in her cheeks as she choked the words back—this bombshell to shatter all peace in the quiet dining room! Something that, if it was to be said at all, should have been said long ago. She could see that now—her timid silence committing her to yet more silence. Bewildered and uncertain she had let the moment for honest declaration go by. And that she was still bewildered and uncertain did nothing to add to her poor stock of courage. To thrust herself forward as claimant for property never intended for her, willed away from her mother deliberately by a woman who would have had nothing but hatred for her mother's child. . . . No, that was something she would never be insensitive enough to do! Mrs. Costello's dark hints of a court case, too; Randy fighting for an inheritance lost to him only by the accident of a missing document that might still be found. In sheer young inexperience, Cathleen's spirit wavered before all these complications. Much better to let matters drift, and in simple truth, constituted as she was, it was impossible for her to do anything else.

With a sigh Randy flung the last of the hastily opened bills onto the breakfast table. ''Mrs. Callaghan sent a boy around this morning to say she can manage to contrive a room for you now,'' he brought out in a casually cheerful tone.

The announcement, so suddenly and unexpectedly made, struck ice at Cathleen's heart. So this was the end! Here was the dreaded dismissal. Her visit to Castle Osborne was over. Bleakness such as she had never imagined stretched ahead of her. *But all my life will be like this,* she thought in hot, young misery. Randy Kilmoran was nothing to her . . . she was less than nothing to him. That was something to which she must adjust herself. All the worry about the will and the inheritance faded before the sense of tragic emptiness that now possessed her. She felt quite weak with the pain of it; so that Randy's voice seemed to come from a distance, saying that he had told Mrs. Callaghan's messenger that Miss Trenton wouldn't be leaving the Castle just yet.

"I took it upon myself to decide for you," the lilting, lazy voice went on. "Knowing the congestion at the Angler's, I can only imagine that Mrs. Callaghan has fixed up a shakedown for herself in some outhouse and would be putting you in the basement room she sleeps in during the season."

Looking up with the numbing pain still dazing her, Cathleen met the cool gray eyes and sudden color flooded her cheeks. That painful tentative fluttering hope—too sharp almost to be borne! Was it that Randy didn't *want* her to go away?

"Did I do wrong?" he asked, with so unusual an air of humility that it was like wine firing her blood.

"Of course not, it was wonderful of you. I *love* being here!" Had she spoken too passionately, too revealingly? Just for an instant the gray eyes watching her darkened and deepened. The mask of nonchalance was gone. Like a flicker of flame, warmth, life . . . something more touched the somberly handsome face. Then quickly as it had come the light died; the mask was in place again.

"That's all right, then," Randy said evenly. "Only that you have had a peculiar sort of visit so far; gloomy enough with its death and funeral to make even Mrs. Callaghan's cellar seem preferable. Now we must see what we can do to brighten things up a bit for you; maybe we could go out sailing on the lough today. We could perhaps," he continued in a musing tone, "land at a couple of the islands and see if we can find a trace of Lanty's poteen still. . . ."

"If you really wanted to go on the lough for some definite purpose like that," Cathleen began earnestly. "I mean . . .

please don't think you have to give up your valuable time to entertaining me, Mr. Kilmoran.''

"Mr. Kilmoran!" he mocked softly. "My name is Randy. . . ."

Cathleen went very pink again. "Randy," she echoed tentatively.

"Randal, to be more formal. But no one with any respect for my feelings ever hands me that laborious tag. . . ."

"What I was going to say," Cathleen persisted doggedly, "is that if you are kind enough to keep me on here I don't want you to put yourself out for me one little bit. I can amuse myself . . . or, better still, isn't there something I could do to help you?" She broke off, wide-eyed, radiant, her lovely, sensitive, little face alight with sudden enthusiasm—this feeling of personal responsibility, of being somehow passionately involved in every facet of the life of this house and all its problems. In the relief of knowing she was not yet to be sent away, a surge of sheer possessive love assailed her. During the brief moment just now when departure had loomed, it had seemed to her that it was the thought of Randy that held her. Now she knew there were other and more complex impulses involved. She didn't want to leave Castle Osborne ever. It was her home as Petunia Road had never been. She belonged to this place with every fiber of her being.

The discovery left her shaken but curiously elated. Ideas, plans . . . that must have been secretly waiting in some hidden part of her mind came rushing through now—as though she had opened a door for them.

"That clover field of yours," she said on a sudden, indefinable impulse. In her urgency she was leaning across the table now. "It's only a suggestion, I know, and maybe you'll think I've got a frightful nerve to be making it . . . but it seems such a shame for that lovely grass to be wasted. Even if you can't put your dream Herefords in there this summer, aren't there any other animals around the place who might be having the benefit of it?''

He stared at her for an instant in sheer blank amazement. Then laughter twinkled in the gray eyes. ''There's a flock of greedy geese in the farmyard who would no doubt nibble it down for me and blow themselves out of shape in the process. . . .''

She refused to be sidetracked by this facetiousness. ''You could *rent* it, turn it into money that way. It seems tragic for it just to lie there unused.''

''It is tragic.'' He was serious once more, and his voice held a note of something like uneasiness, asking, ''But was it in Petunia Road you learned this concern for the tragedies of wasted land?''

''I don't know.'' Young and candid, the very blue eyes looked squarely across the table. ''It's something land teaches you very quickly—if you have the love of land in your blood. When you stand on a hillside as we did the other night and look out over a great estate . . . the good land and the bad land lying there waiting for the things you can do to it; when you see the way things grow and thrive with attention . . . the gifts each season holds out to you . . . gifts waiting to be taken. . . .'' She broke off, breathless, curiously excited, suddenly aware of the odd way in which Randy was staring at her.

He said slowly, ''I thought one had to be Irish to have this passion for land in the abstract. . . .''

''My mother was Irish,'' Cathleen confided in a burst of recklessness.

''Oh, well that accounts for lots of things, doesn't it? Your Celtic coloring . . . those eyes . . . that hair.'' Something subtly insinuating in the way he spoke was to return to Cathleen later. But now, hurrying on, she was only interested in all that she had to say.

"Those strawberries and currants in the kitchen garden, too, couldn't we pick them and sell them to the hotels in Osbornestown and Dunbarragh? It's absolutely criminal to let the birds have all that fruit just for the lack of a little enterprise. If you haven't got a market van, you have at least got a car. We could lead it up this morning—"

"You mean you are willing to pick fruit for two or three hours on end . . . the most back-breaking form of toil ever invented?" His tone was puzzled. "Just why should you be so . . . altruistic . . . I wonder?"

"Some streak of thrift in me, I suppose. I just can't bear to see things wasted . . . and it isn't as if the Castle Osborne estate was exactly wealthy. I mean, whoever inherits this place ultimately, it is surely all to the good that this fruit harvest should be gathered in and sold profitably." She stopped short, half-scared at her own boldness. Hadn't she had too much . . . overstepped most glaringly the decent reticences of the mere disinterested guest?

Randy stood up. "Well," he brought out on a long, slowly exhaled breath, as though he didn't quite know what to make of her. But whatever he was thinking, his glance remained impassive as he agreed in a matter-of-fact tone that her suggestion was an extremely practical one.

Enthusiasm seemed to take hold of him then as he began to plan the day's campaign. There were at least half a dozen hotels within reach, packed at this season with summer visitors and ready to buy any garden produce he could offer. "All we have to do," he said, "is to fill all the chip baskets we can find . . . there used to be piles of them in the old loft over the storehouse in the garden." He went to the window and called Mollie in, telling her of their project.

"You've got to do a hard day's work for once in your life," he ended with brotherly ferocity, "and you can thank Cathleen for it. It was her idea."

Cathleen. He had never used her Christian name before and the sound of it now so casually spoken made her pulse beat unevenly.

"But it's a wonderful idea," Mollie was agreeing warmly. "We ought to have thought of it ourselves . . . only that it is a little difficult to realize that we *may* pick the fruit—and sell it; now that poor old grandam isn't here anymore with her old-fashioned notions that selling things out of the garden is a disgrace."

After that it was all very simply and friendly—and extremely strenuous. Stooping over the strawberry beds under the sultry gray sky they worked steadily, until even Mollie was too exhausted to chatter anymore and Yo-Yo, who had spent a blissful hour pouncing at their hands and feet among the overgrown leaves, collapsed in an attitude of conscious and self-pitying exhaustion in the middle of a cluster of pinks.

Filling her chip baskets in the silence of that last weary half hour before lunch, it came to Cathleen that this was one of the most satisfying mornings she had ever known in her life—this lavish, lovely garden with its rich fruits and good rows of sturdy kitchen vegetables, the winding paths between their clipped box edging, the gnarled apple trees dreaming under the quiet Irish sky; old Danny the gardener murmuring to himself as he went about his tasks like a contented bumblebee, an old, old man who remembered with love a child in a sunbonnet who had played at his feet in summers long dead. How it all held her with its hints of mysteriously familiar association. It wasn't going to be easy to leave Castle Osborne.

But maybe I won't have to leave! The thought came unbidden; sharply disturbing with its promise of an ecstasy that was half pain. Oh, if only the muddle about the will could work out in some wonderful way so that nobody need be hurt, thought Cathleen, and her mind began to riot with wild imaginary solutions. The will could be found . . . a new will written by

Lady FitzOsborne miraculously on her deathbed—leaving half the estate to Randy and half to the granddaughter she had at the last moment recognized and loved. Or, the will was not found, but somehow the inefficient Mr. Philligan could stumble upon the fact of Sheila Costello's second marriage, her death and the existence of her daughter. Picking strawberries with feverish intensity, Cathleen saw herself honored and acclaimed; Mr. Philligan in his white raincoat begging her to take possession of the lands that were her heritage, while she demurred that in deference to her grandmother's known wishes Randy must have his share.

There was, of course, yet another solution! But she didn't dare to let herself think about that. It was too crazy, too heavenly, too altogether impossible, and Randy's voice calling to her sharply from the far side of the vast strawberry bed somehow shattered completely the poor little shadow of a dream that was almost too timid to be a dream at all.

It was lunchtime, he was announcing with the asperity of a tired and hungry man, and they had enough fruit gathered to feed the entire population of Dunbarragh for a week.

"Not that we have by any means cleared these currant bushes," Cathleen pointed out as they walked through the green lane back to the house.

Randy groaned. "Is there nothing you'd leave for the birds of the air?" he teased. "Don't tell me you had an Irish mother after this! I'm thinking it's Scots she must have been, skinflint Scots from Aberdeen!" But the warmth in his gray eyes told her he was pleased with her . . . pleased with the good morning's work.

"*Did* you have an Irish mother?" Mollie inquired, with quick interest. "What part of Ireland did she come from?"

"She died when I was born," Cathleen answered evasively. "I . . . knew so little about her. . . ."

A statement pitiful enough in its implications to render even the chatterbox Mollie aware of the impossibility of asking further questions. But feeling as though she had stepped back just in time from the edge of a dangerous precipice Cathleen was uneasy all through lunch. What a fool she had been ever to mention her mother at all!

The trip into Dunbarragh that afternoon, however, banished her forebodings. It was all so gay and friendly. Randy in an uproarious mood driving from hotel to hotel with his wares and when the last basket of fruit had been disposed of, treating the girls to a lavish dinner at the last hotel of call, which must have made serious inroads into the day's profits!

Driving home through the twilight they saw the daylight fade over the western mountain peaks and the full moon come up over the lough. Vast and mysterious the silvery water shone, the dark tree-covered islands clearly visible, yet unreal and insubstantial in that fairy light. So warm and still was the air that not a ripple disturbed that calm and shining surface, not the smallest wave broke by the verge of the sandy shore road along which they drove.

"We could go for a swim, it's that quiet tonight," Mollie suggested, and Randy seized on the notion with a zest that seemed to surprise her.

"You have never put foot in the water if you can help it!" she marveled.

"Well, I feel like it tonight . . . and Cathleen hasn't had a chance of a swim since she came; more shame to us!" was Randy's forthright reply. "Go on upstairs now and get your togs," he ordered the girls in his autocratic way as they reached the house.

On the upper landing Mollie paused at her own door, her eyes speculatively fixed on Cathleen. "I've never known Randy the way he is tonight . . . the way he has been all day," she said, in a puzzled tone. You'd think with the worry over the lost will . . . the two of us not knowing if we'll have a roof over our heads this time next week, he'd be, well, a bit sobered. But he seems so lighthearted. It's as though some great load had been lifted off his mind.''

''Maybe he is feeling cheery because we picked all that fruit and sold it so successfully,'' Cathleen suggested.

Mollie shook her head. ''It's more than that. I know Randy. Something important has happened to make him so cock-a-hoop. It's not just selling that fruit.'' The green eyes were very bright peering at Cathleen in the eerie moonlight that was the landing's only illumination. ''Maybe it's *you*!'' the child said softly. ''He likes you. He wouldn't let you go back to Mrs. Callaghan's this morning. He planned that dinner in Dunbarragh for you this evening . . . now he wants to go swimming with you. I've never known him bother this much over any other girl—as a rule he avoids females . . . keeps out of their way. I . . . believe he's keen on you!''

Cathleen went crimson. ''What utter nonsense!'' she exclaimed heatedly, her heart beginning to pound uncomfortably against her ribs. ''The reason we had dinner in Dunbarragh was that we were too late to have it here, and as for the swimming, it is the obvious thing to do this warm, moonlit night. If Randy did suggest it specially for me it is simply because he is being kind . . . and a good host.''

Mollie smiled her elfish smile. ''I expect that's it,'' she agreed demurely—and so utterly without conviction that Cathleen moved on with an exasperated shrug. Mollie was a menace with her wonderful green eyes and chattering tongue. Why shouldn't Randy be happy today? Remember her own mood of elation this morning . . . remembering, too, that moment when over the breakfast table the gray eyes had looked at her with a hot, quick flame in their depths, Cathleen's pulse fluttered. ''He likes you . . . I've never known him bother this much over any other girl. . . .'' Supposing that was the truth! Not just the romantic imagining of a sentimental schoolgirl sister. Ecstasy touched Cathleen's heart, wild and unbidden, so that she caught her breath sharply.

Entering her room still dazed by the moment's emotion, she stood staring stupidly at the woman who hovered by the dressing table, turning in hurried guilt to face her. Mrs. Costello!

"What is it? What do you want?" Cathleen asked, with a stab of fear.

"I've just been doing your room, miss. 'Twas a good chance, I thought, to clean the place up a bit and you away to Dunbarragh for the evening."

But you don't turn rooms out without dusters or brushes, Cathleen thought, looking at the woman's empty hands. Had Mrs. Costello simply and brazenly been going through her possessions?

"I took that old picture of the drowning woman away, miss," the sly, soft voice went on. "It was there above the fireplace this ten years or more and it is all soiled with the damp and the flies. So I gave you another picture. . . ."

Something in Mrs. Costello's tone made Cathleen turn quickly to the mantelpiece, and there in an oasis of candlelight where the religious oleograph had hung was a portrait in oils . . . a girl with dark curling hair and the very blue eyes under their smoky lashes, so like Cathleen's own eyes looking back at her that she could feel all the blood drain slowly from her heart.

"Who is it?" she forced herself to ask in a dry thread of a whisper. But even before Mrs. Costello spoke she knew what the answer would be . . . and why the picture had been hung there.

CHAPTER SIX

FOR A LONG MOMENT there was silence, and, in that measuring of glances, such hatred looked out of the old woman's eyes that involuntarily Cathleen shuddered.

" 'Tis Miss Sheila as she was the age of eighteen." The words came out flat, passionless, yet with a hint of sinister significance.

"She was . . . pretty," Cathleen whispered, forcing herself to look once more at the softly colored painting. That face so exactly like her own that to look at it was almost the same as being confronted by a mirror! The curling black hair framing the contours of the wide pure brow, the deep blue eyes with their smudge of thick dark lashes, the young red mouth with the full slightly cleft lower lip . . . inescapable, that final characteristic! In the uncolored studio photograph of her mother—the only picture Cathleen had so far seen—these similarities had not been so clear, nor the resemblance between mother and daughter so striking. This oil portrait proclaimed it . . . positively screamed it! That, of course, was why Mrs. Costello had produced it.

She knows who I am . . . she has known all along, Cathleen thought in an access of panic as she rummaged for her swim suit in a drawer so chaotic that it was obvious Mrs. Costello had indeed been surprised in the middle of investigating its contents.

Dragging out the white woolen swimsuit, Cathleen stood hesitant. Downstairs Randy and Mollie would be impatiently awaiting her, but magnetized by the horror of the situation, she could not move . . . could not bear to leave the room until something more revealing had been said. What exactly *was* Mrs. Costello's game? Was she going to come into the open now with her knowledge of the stranger's identity? It seemed that she was not. Cat and mouse tactics were, probably, more in her line than direct attack. Hands folded over her shrunken breast, her head a little on one side, she stood in mock humility, a slow smile curving her withered lips. "Aye, she was pretty . . . the girl who ruined our poor Michael's life; looking at her there in the fine picture, you can hardly wonder at him sacrificing himself for her."

"Sacrificing himself!" Indignation swept discretion to the winds. If Mrs. Costello enjoyed oblique references—two could play at that game! "I should think Miss FitzOsborne was the one who did the sacrificing," Cathleen said coldly. "To give up her home, her heritage for the sake of a . . . penniless young drunkard . . . ."

Mrs. Costello's eyes flashed, but the crooked smile did not waver. "Aye . . . she gave up her heritage, right enough . . . and there's no scheming and twisting and hiding of rightful wills that will get it back for her . . . or her children." Such venom gleamed in the old hooded eyes now, that Cathleen involuntarily moved a step nearer to the door. But controlling her nerves she forced herself to linger in the dim candlelit room, filled with its wavering shadows, its atmosphere of dark, unspoken hatreds.

This woman is dangerous . . . I must not let her see I am afraid of her! Like cold water flung revivingly in her face the thought brought fresh courage to Cathleen. "You think Lady FitzOsborne's will has been hidden somewhere, then?" she brought out in just the right tone of detached interest.

"I'm sure of it. That's why I'm day and night searching for it. And I'll find it!" Mrs. Costello's voice rose to a hysterical shriek. "As God is in heaven I'll see that the orders herself gave for the disposal of her property are obeyed. To Mr. Randy she willed it—and there was justice in that, for it was the Kilmorans Miss Sheila defrauded when she ran away on her wedding eve. If she had married the man her mother chose for her—Mr. Terence Kilmoran, her Ladyship's own cousin—''

''You mean old Lady FitzOsborne was a Kilmoran?'' Cathleen brought out in an astonishment that for the moment swamped everything else.

''She was indeed. Kilmoran was her maiden name, and though it was an aristocratic family she came from, it was even at that time without substance. 'Twas in the old days of the Land League war that the Kilmoran mansion was looted and burned in the County Meath, and after that the family was scattered. Herself was landless and penniless when she married Sir John FitzOsborne, and he twenty years older than herself. Seventeen she was and a lovely spirited girl . . . God rest her! 'Twas then I came to her service, and myself the one age as her. She'd talk to me the way girls do talk, telling me of the pride she had in this great place, and how she would give her first son Kilmoran as a Christian name. 'He'll build up the family again, Mary, the way it used to be,' she'd say to me.'' Pausing, Mrs. Costello wiped a tear from her cheek.

''And there was no son born to her,'' Cathleen put in softly, moved in spite of herself by this story of broken human hopes and wounded pride.

''There was no sign of a child at all for the half of a lifetime, and a terrible bitterness came on my lady. All the time I was bearing my own childer—ten of them there were—I used to be praying for her. And then . . . I'll never forget the joy there was when those prayers seemed to be answered. But it was as though God made a mock of us.'' The old voice faltered, then rallied suddenly on a note of defiance like the echo of that strong and undefeated spirit of whom she spoke. '' 'Twas with the girl child in the bed beside her that she planned the marriage that would yet retrieve her dream; the girl child must take the name of Kilmoran in matrimony . . . bring back the old glories that way. And when Miss Sheila grew up to wreck this last poor hope . . . what did herself do but take Randy Kilmoran into this house along with her and make him like her own son. She was a great and a brave fighter. A Kilmoran she remained in her heart to the day of her death, and now . . . a Kilmoran shall rule this place in her stead. That is why I have made up my mind to find the will—if it is to be found—giving Mr. Randy his rights in the sight of God and the blessed dead.''

Something in the pointed way this final tirade was flung at her set Cathleen's nerves on edge, so that she said, with some asperity, ''A very laudable determination, Mrs. Costello. But you will hardly find the missing will in my chest of drawers . . . I dislike having my personal possessions disturbed and raked around in my absence. If you want to search for the will in this room will you kindly wait another time until I am here to help you?''

Mrs. Costello gave an abashed little snort of laughter. A pitiful, undignified sound robbing her suddenly of all her menace. She was no more than a cringing old woman then, nervously fingering her shawl, saying in quavering apology, ''Indeed then, miss, you have a right to be annoyed . . . but I do be half-mad when I begin hunting for that same will. Any drawer or cupboard I see foreninst me, I have to go looking through it. 'Twas no offense to yourself I meant, coming in here turning your things around with no real hopes of the will being in it. For how could it be here, and you a young lady from London—a total stranger to us, that could have no connection of any kind with the sorrows of this poor, ill-fated house?''

Cathleen gave it up at that. They were back where they had started, and she was as far away as ever from having discovered just what was in Mrs. Costello's sly and tortuous mind. Running down the shadowy moonlit staircase, she summed the matter up, hurriedly pushing back into the recesses of her mind the strange story of a lifetime's scheming to which she had just listened; a scheming for land and possessions to which all human feeling had been sacrificed. What was it in the Irish nature that made them this way about land? This love for the soil and stones of their country that amounted almost to idolatry. Hadn't she sensed it in Randy . . . sensed it even in herself? With a shiver she turned her thoughts to Mrs. Costello. Undoubtedly the old woman had recognized her. Why, then, didn't she speak out? Perhaps, because in her ignorant and helpless fashion she lacked the courage to issue the final fantastic challenge. Or, she wasn't a hundred percent certain and had hoped the production of the painting would have startled the stranger into betraying herself.

But I betrayed nothing, Cathleen congratulated herself, as she hurried through the sleeping flower garden with Mollie—who had waited for her. Randy with manlike impatience had gone on ahead and could even now be seen plunging into the moonlit water that glimmered beyond the ghostly trees. Watching him strike out purposefully, his arms rising and falling in powerful rhythm, Cathleen drew in a sharp, quick breath. The things Mollie had said just now—and which had been banished for the time by Mrs. Costello's strange behavior: "He likes you . . . I believe he's keen on you!" Even to hear it spoken in teenage silliness was like listening to music and the blare of golden, triumphant trumpets.

With trembling hands she unfastened her dress and fumbled with shoe laces, while Mollie, already undressed, danced by the water's edge. "Oh, hurry . . . do hurry!" the little girl urged. "Randy will swim on and on and we shall never catch up with him."

Cathleen said, in a tranced voice, "I can't hurry. Go on without me. I don't mind."

With a flash of childishly thin white legs and arms Mollie went, running into the warm shallow water that filled the little bay that lay within the curve of the dock. Left alone Cathleen gave herself up to the magic all around her . . . and that deeper, more subtle magic within her tempestuous heart. This night of unearthy beauty—it was something she would remember as long as she lived; black hills folded against a night-blue sky, islands and trees and sleeping flowers etched darkly in shadow, caught here and there like silver filigree by the brilliant rays of the moon. The air smelled of crushed wet rushes and wild mint, of mild milky lake water and peaty mud. Clad in her brief white swimsuit she walked slowly to the edge of the dock, feeling the warm sweet air soft as a caress against her body. With a little shiver of sensuous delight she stood poised to dive, her face lifted for an instant to the sky where, high and serene, the full moon rode above the banked soft clouds. Randy had turned to swim toward her now, his voice calling across the wide space of water some bantering words she could not make out . . . only that she knew he was watching her, waiting for her to come out to him. Putting arms together, she drew a deep breath, and it was just as she was about to surrender herself to the embrace of the shining water that a furry bundle flung itself at her feet, her cry of alarm reducing the moment to absurdity.

"It's Yo-Yo," she called out in exasperation to Mollie, as she tried to shake the little cat off. Sitting up on his haunches he had clasped his paws—with claws carefully sheathed—around her leg, apparently under the impression that he was saving her life. "He has followed us. He doesn't want me to dive in! He's hanging on to me!" shrieked Cathleen.

"Well, slap him," advised Mollie. "Shake him off."

Cathleen looked down at the dark monkeyish face with its curiously human eyes. "Go home, Yo-Yo," she urged. "Go home at once, bad cat!" Making a soft crooning sound Yo-Yo stretched himself up on his hind legs and hooked a claw purposefully into the woolen swimsuit. Lifting him up Cathleen fondled him a moment, then putting him down firmly with a further order to go home, she plunged into the lake. How soft the water was . . . like cool, floating silk, holding her up, making her body feel light, and pure and empty so that her spirit soared up and away; all the jangled impressions of the day slipping away from her, leaving her calm and free. Using the breaststroke she swam, hardly disturbing the water, moonlight pouring down on her uplifted face. Yo-Yo was a nuisance, howling behind her on the dock, his desolate cries rising loud and wild in the quiet night.

"He's going to dive! He has dived!" yelled Mollie in alarm, and turning, Cathleen saw the tiny seallike head forging through the water toward them.

"He'll drown," moaned Mollie, setting off vigorously in the direction of her dauntless pet.

Treading water Cathleen watched the little drama of rescue, and Randy, who had reached her side now, called out to Mollie standing in the shallows with the dripping kitten in her arms, "Take him home and dry him if you don't want him to die of pneumonia. . . . And don't bother to come back!" he added in brotherly dismissal.

"Poor brave little Yo-Yo—fancy his trying to follow us!" Cathleen murmured, trying not to find any significance in Randy's final injunction to his sister.

"He's a game little animal, right enough," Randy agreed. "But Siamese are game, more like dogs. I'm told I can train him to retrieve—take him hunting with me when I go shooting. How far do you want to swim?" he was asking then, and after that there was nothing in the world that mattered to either of them but their smooth progress through the moonlit water. In silence they went, Randy matching his stroke to Cathleen's, so that she moved without haste, easily, luxuriously.

"Think you could get as far as that first island?" he asked presently, and, because she was intoxicated with the moment and its wordless implications, Cathleen agreed that the island was well within her reach. But she had forgotten how out of practice she was with her swimming and hadn't in the least realized how far the island really was. By the time they had been swimming for ten minutes the water had grown strangely cold and was somehow less buoyant. Her breath began to come with difficulty and her temples throbbed. Now, no matter how slowly Randy went, she was lagging behind and presently the moonlight went black and the strangest buzzing sounded in her ears. After that she wasn't quite sure what happened—only that Randy's arms were around her and he was carrying her through shallow water, to the island, laying her on a bank of warm dry pine needles that had a lovely smell.

In a moment or two she was herself again, sitting up, apologizing for her weakness as Randy chafed her cold hands. His face bent over her looked so drawn and concerned, and she could see the great smooth muscles moving under the skin of his naked shoulders as he worked. "I'm all right!" she assured him. "I can't think why I was so silly ... only that the water seemed all at once cold."

"I shouldn't have made you come so far!" His tone was abject with contrition, and looking at the distant shore Cathleen began to wonder with a small pang of concern how she was ever to accomplish the return journey! But as though he had read her thoughts Randy was saying that he would swim back and fetch the small rowing boat that was always ready, tied to an iron ring in the wall of the little dock.

"Just lie there and rest," he ordered her gently, "and I'll be back for you in a couple of ticks."

It was very quiet on the island when he had left her. For a while she lay listening to the rhythmical splash-splash of his going, then there was no sound at all, only the tiny sighs and stirrings of the trees all around her. Still exhausted by her foolish collapse, she felt dreamy and unreal. Nothing seemed to matter greatly. A drowsy happiness that she was far too dazed to explore filled her heart, and after a while she could hear the rattle of oars on oarlocks, and Randy was back again, dressed once more in his old tweed suit.

"I brought your towel and things," he said, flinging the bundle onto the ground beside her. "Thought you'd be cold sitting around in your wet togs. I'll tootle around in the boat a few minutes while you dress . . . give me a shout when you are ready."

She liked the matter-of-fact way he made this tactful arrangement, not joking over it fatuously as some men would have done. But there was so much she liked about Randy! Rubbing her shivering body in the big comfortable towel, life began to take shape and substance again, and when she was dressed and warm a soft swift excitement flowed over her. Calling to Randy to come to her, feeling his hard calloused hand crushing her fingers as he helped her into the boat, she gave herself up to the moment's exquisite and mindless joy. He had taken off his jacket now and wrapped it around her shoulders. He had produced from somewhere a packet of chocolate, which she ate with a sudden hollow sense of hunger. After the chocolate she declared herself completely restored, and leaning back in the stern of the little boat, she watched Randy row with slow powerful strokes.

They talked first about the island they had just left, Cathleen wondering if it might be the island on which Lanty Conor brewed his poteen. But Randy didn't think so. Lanty would go farther afield if he was really running an illicit still. "One of these days when we feel like it, we'll take the yacht and sail out into the center of the lough where the really remote islands are," he said.

Cathleen liked the easy natural way he made his plan, as though there was all the time in the world for them to go exploring the great sheet of water. *As though I were never going away*, she thought, trailing her fingers in the moon-colored ripples folded back like bright wings on either side of the boat. She was remembering with a sudden pang of discomfort Mrs. Costello's enmity, but there was no time to dwell on it, for Randy was asking her where she did her swimming in London.

"In the local swimming pools mostly. It is only when we go to the seaside in the summer that I get any real distances to cover. That's why I put up such a poor show tonight." The thought of Bognor came to her then . . . and Len Cranton, poor Len who had taught her to dive last year! He had been so patient with her—so careful, knowing to a fraction just how much she could do, never allowing her to tire herself or stay in the water too long. How horrified he would have been if he had seen her setting out to swim across this stretch of cold lough water tonight!

"Who is 'we'," Randy asked suddenly in his uncompromising way, and something in the penetrating almost hostile way he looked at her made Cathleen feel that he could see the thought that was Len floating around above her head!

"My people," she murmured. "We go to Bognor most years . . . my stepmother, stepbrothers and stepsisters—the only relations I have in the world, really. My father is dead. . . ."

"And your Irish mother?"

Cathleen nodded. "Yes, she is dead, too." How easy it would be, she thought on a sudden surge of almost unspeakable relief, to tell him all the rest now . . . at this moment; here on the peaceful moonlit lake where they were alone—and happy. He had been so kind and friendly all day; perhaps more than friendly! And now the gray eyes were softening as they looked at her, the grim impassive young face seemed carved in lines of unfamiliar gentleness. "And you didn't go to Bognor this year," he said softly, "you came to Castle Osborne!"

"Yes," she echoed in a hushed little voice, "I came to Castle Osborne." It was as though in that whispered exchange much more than the actual words had been spoken. Resting on his oars, leaning toward her, Randy looked long and questioningly into her eyes. Unwaveringly she met his glance, her breath fluttering through her parted lips and a sense of sweet surrender came to her. Beginning to row again, he was singing quietly to himself, a lilting swinging air with strange words to it.

Listening to the deep, easy voice, Cathleen searched in her mind for the phrases with which to begin her confession. Surely he would understand how strange her position was, how difficult it had been to speak out. He would realize the series of accidents that had brought her to Castle Osborne, and how in her inexperience she had not known what to do when confronted by the dramatic happenings of the past ten days. And she would explain that she spoke now simply to save Mr. Philligan the expense of his continued search for her mother. She would tell Randy that she felt her grandmother's wishes ought to be carried out—that she made no claim on the estate. Surely he would be glad then . . . not angry with her for her timid silence!

"Randy!" she began in a small choked voice . . . but he was still singing, gazing out over the water, his face dreamy and lost . . . as though he had forgotten her presence.

"Is that a Gaelic song?" she asked when the final stanza ended, because it seemed a little impolite not to make some comment on his singing.

" 'Tis an old Munster love song," Randy said, and started to translate it for her:

I am a young fellow that ran out of my land and means,
And my mother at home wouldn't give me a wife or gains,
I placed my affection on one that had gold in store,
And I promised that colleen from her I'd part no more.

Cathleen's eyes widened unhappily as she listened to these quaint words . . . and quainter sentiments; so curiously apposite that she found them indefinably frightening.

"Land and love," she said, "are they always mixed up in Irish romance?"

Randy laughed. "I hadn't thought about it; but I suppose most of the love songs of Munster and Connaught do contain a bit of healthy peasant bartering."

They had reached the dock now, and stepping ashore, Cathleen felt as though she moved into another and more austere world leaving her mood of mindless joy behind. And yet there was magic enough as they walked through the larch wood, the pale globes of hydrangea blossom banked on either side of them. Randy had placed a hand under her elbow to steady her going, for the path was threaded through with the wandering roots of conifers, treacherous for unwary feet in that dim green twilight. She must make her confession now . . . quickly, before they reached the house. "Randy!" she began again, but suddenly his hand tightened on her arm, and he was drawing her back into the bushes with a warning, "Hush!" Footsteps she heard then, hurried and furtive, and in a patch of brilliant moonlight she could see the bright hair of Lanty Conor.

"He's making for the boat," Randy whispered. "Let's watch and see what he is up to!"

Pressed close against Randy's side behind the pale flowers with their faint ghostly fragrance, Cathleen tried to think about Lanty Conor, and failed utterly. She could only think about Randy . . . the rough tweed jacket on which her cheek rested, the hard young arm that somehow had arranged itself so easily around her shoulders. Only that there was no joy in this sudden, secretive contact . . . fear stirring the depths of her heart, a choking blinding fear! Because it had occurred to her that in a few moments she would be back in her bedroom where the all-revealing oil painting of Sheila awaited her. And all at once, with the thought of that telltale picture, came the flash of revelation that illuminated so many small faces of the long day—the things Mollie had said of Randy's lightheartedness, "as though some great load had been lifted off his mind;" the look he had given her when she had told him of her Irish mother, and the queer little song he had sung to her just now . . . every word of it fitting so cold-bloodedly and calculatingly into their own story.

Lanty was slithering into the boat now, packing in something that looked like a butter churn, picking up the oars and pushing away from the side. Cathleen could feel the long sigh with which Randy relaxed as he observed these developments . . . feel, too, the sudden pounding of his heart as, Lanty Conor forgotten, he swept her into his arms. And it was even as his lips came down on her own that she thought, *but there is no need for any confession . . . he knows who I am. How could he have lived for two years in the same house as that picture, which is like my own picture—and not know?*

CHAPTER SEVEN

IT WASN'T a very successful kiss, rough and impetuous on Randy's part, while Cathleen, rigid with horror, shrank from his embrace. In a moment he had released her with a muffled, rather angry, "Sorry! I ought not to have done that."

"It's all right," she murmured wretchedly as they moved on. But it wasn't all right, and her stiffly muttered words did nothing to make it so.

"I'm not only a young fellow who ran out of his land and means, but I seem to have lost my mind into the bargain!" Randy offered in a miserable attempt to laugh the whole thing off. "Put it down to the moon," he said.

If only she could! And how dare he remind her of that dreadful cynical song? "I placed my affection on one that had gold in store!" What could be plainer? As though he were trying to tell her that, even if she were the missing heiress who would dispossess him, he had no intention of letting Castle Osborne slip out of his grasp. Perhaps he had been struck by her likeness to the lost Sheila as far back as that night in the Euston mail train. But after a moment's thought Cathleen dismissed this possibility as unlikely. He would hardly have wanted her at the castle if he had suspected her identity then. It was much more likely that the extraordinary coincidence of her resemblance to the FitzOsborne family had dawned on him gradually . . . and then, like Mrs. Costello, he might not be a hundred percent sure, fitting the little bits of evidence in here and there, keeping her at the castle so that he could watch her closely.

No doubt they would have compared notes, he and Mrs. Costello, and Mr. Philligan would have been sent to Dublin to check up on the whole thing more exactly . . . perhaps he had not gone to Dublin at all, but to London! Perhaps even now he was hammering at the door of the house in Petunia Road!

Trudging along at Randy's side in awkward silence, Cathleen's brain seethed. The way he had looked at her this morning when she had told him her mother had been Irish. He had said, "That accounts for lots of things." And then he had suddenly become so lighthearted that even Mollie had noticed it, saying he behaved as though some great load had been lifted. *Perhaps,* Cathleen thought, *he thinks I have no knowledge of my mother's ancestors . . . that is why he has not yet challenged me with the relationship.* She remembered how evasively she had answered Mollie's questions on the way back from the strawberry picking, saying she knew nothing about the mother who had died at her birth. Or perhaps he was not angry because there was no use being angry, and he had already decided to try to marry her . . . for the sake of the estate. Just as Lady FitzOsborne had married her Sir John. The landless Kilmoran's fighting for something that was far more important to them than love!

He said suddenly—breaking the strained silence, "That object Lanty was smuggling into the boat looked to me extraordinarily like a poteen still."

"That churn thing?"

"Yes, a worm, they call it. Wish to heavens I had the authority to sack that fellow! A nice thing it will be for Castle Osborne if we have a police raid on the lough, and they find a working still on one of our islands."

"A police raid," she murmured bemusedly, and he began to tell her about the raids—made usually in the dead of night and the arrests and fines and even imprisonments that resulted for those who were caught red-handed. "Sometimes there is a spot of shooting,'' he ended cheerfully. She could feel him watching her anxiously as he talked—as though he were trying to think of some way he could get back into her good graces. She knew she seemed heavy and sulky, but for the life of her she could not pretend to be anything else just now.

In the big gloomy hall she would have broken away from him and hurried upstairs, but he caught both her hands and held them tightly. Small and icy and submissive they rested in his powerful grasp and her face lifted to his was white and wan.

"I've half-killed you with that long swim," he mourned. "And I've annoyed you, Cathleen. I'm sorry. I know that kiss was a mistake . . . that this is no time in my affairs to go falling in love . . . me, without a penny to my name; no job, no home." He laughed bitterly. "Only that love doesn't wait for things like that!"

"Don't!" she cried brokenly. "Please don't say any more." Wrenching her hands away from him she fled. Love! Oh, but it was unbearable that he should talk to her of love! Running into her room she locked the door behind her and flung herself down on her bed, and a fit of violent weeping seized her. For a little while today she had been so happy . . . and tonight on the lough in the moonlight it had all been so wonderful. Randy seemed so tender in his big awkward way . . . as though he were not used to tenderness, offering it tentatively . . . almost experimentally. Which just about described the situation! A Randy with no use for girls suddenly trying to turn himself into a gallant lover. Oh, it was all so clear, so horrible!

Pressing her wet face into the pillows Cathleen felt as though her heart must break. Randy! Randy! If only she had not at first believed in him . . . if only she had not been such a simple, credulous fool; letting herself imagine that an unknown girl from a London suburb could mean anything to this man whose whole life and every passion was bound up in the possessing of

Castle Osborne. And now it was as though one part of her stood aside, understanding his obsession with property, sympathizing with it . . . even in some insane fashion approving of it! How easy it would have been for him if she had drowned out there on the loch when exhaustion overcame her! But suspicion had reached its ultimate hell in that frightful thought . . . frightened and sickened she thrust it away from her, feeling as if she were going mad.

Somewhere a clock struck reminding her that it was midnight. Stiffly she rose from the bed, and with shaking hands groped for matches so that she might light the candles that were her only illumination. Shivering with cold and a strange nausea, she took off her dress, pausing presently in her preparations for the night to hold one flickering candle aloft before the softly colored face above the mantelpiece. Lonely, remote, the blue eyes seemed to look down at her. "Mother!" she whispered brokenly . . . her own loneliness and young desolation flooding her; all the long years of it . . . filled with the fantasies only motherless children know. So that her tired mind slid easily back into the turmoil, half-fact, half-fantasy that now possessed her. She was, at that moment, so far from the point at which truth and imagination can be disentangled, that it was quite simple for her to accept the dark horror of Randy's behavior, simple to see herself identified with the girl looking down at her from a tarnished frame; a girl who had wept for lost love in this very room perhaps, even as she now wept. The ill-fated women of the house of FitzOsborne. Even her grandmothers's tears could shine now through this silent hour, pitiful and purified, demanding her compassion. Through three generations it had been the same—a story of heartbreak and frustration, a story of young lives ruined by the lust for land.

Creeping into bed, shaking from head to foot within the slack embrace of sheets that seemed like ice, Cathleen found herself longing with a pang of unbearable homesickness for the familiar security of her own small bed at home in Petunia Road. Oh, the bliss it would be to find herself safely there this very moment, seeing through prim muslin blinds the streetlight shining through the acacia tree at the end of the front garden—a house full of wholesome cheerful young people—who didn't seem dull to Cathleen anymore, just safe and kind and ordinary. Even the thought of Len Cranton next door began to take on a rosy nostalgic glow; dear Len who was so good, so utterly honest and unselfish. And her stepmother, that firm, sensible most beautifully unimaginative soul, no storms of hatred, no undercurrents of guile disturbing her eternal placidity. What a relief it would be to pour out to her the whole, wild history of this incredible Irish holiday, ask for her counsel and advice. And what, after all, was to prevent her doing this? Cathleen asked herself. She was not a prisoner in Castle Osborne. She would go home tomorrow, she decided, as she began to drift into an uneasy doze. She ought to have gone long ago . . . right away, that troubled day of Lady FitzOsborne's death. It had been crazy to try and battle through this wildnerness of intrigue alone.

But when the morning came, after a night of feverish, terrifying dreams, she woke to find her head throbbing unbearably, her body burning with heat while the icy shivers still raced up and down her shrinking spine. Getting out of bed with some hazy idea of forcing herself to dress and catch the Dunbarragh bus that passed the big gates of the estate soon after eight, she stood groping for her clothes until faintness overcame her and she was compelled to lie down again, compelled to admit to herself that she was really ill. That dangerous interlude when, after her collapse in the water she had lain in her wet swimsuit under the pine trees on the island, had taken its toll. She had caught a chill . . . perhaps pneumonia even, for there was a dull ache in her chest like a heavy iron pressing between her ribs.

Through a haze of fever she saw Mrs. Costello come in with a tray of morning tea; something that had never happened before, a detail of the household routine, no doubt dislocated by the week of the funeral, upset and now resumed. And the thought of a cup of hot tea had never been more welcome! But sitting up to take the tray, the pain in her chest caused Cathleen to cry out and with tears of weakness and despair running down her cheek she sank back onto the pillows.

After that it was all rather confused, a wavering, swaying world through which Mrs. Costello moved with a kindliness and efficiency that might have been surprising if everything had not been so clouded. The gently bustling figure pouring out tea, fetching a hot water bottle, building a fire of turf in the cavernous hearth . . . a voice running on sharp with concern, "Going out swimming in the black of night, playing yourselves out there in the icy water . . . ye ought to have had more sense, the whole three of ye. I'm ashamed of Mr. Randy letting you do it, so I am! And Miss Mollie getting the little cat half-drowned. Isn't it sick this morning, the same as yourself, the creature!"

"You mean Yo-Yo is ill?" Cathleen echoed stupidly, finding some strange gleam of comfort in the fact that old Mrs. Costello could speak so compassionately of the little cat. People who loved animals weren't usually wholly villainous.

"He is indeed," she asserted, kneeling by the smoking reluctant fire. "Isn't he down there in the kitchen in a basket by the fire, sneezing his head off and wheezing, and Miss Mollie out of her mind trying to make him lap a little milk."

Billows of smoke from the fire then absorbed her attention for a while. And presently Cathleen heard her muttering to herself that there must be a rook's nest "within in the chimlee."

"This smoke will ruin the picture above," she said suddenly in a worried tone, and then she was climbing on a chair, taking the oil painting from its nail above the mantelshelf to place it out of harm's way inside the big wardrobe. In vague relief Cathleen watched it disapper. At least she need not lie now confronted by this ghostly likeness of herself with all its tangled implications.

"Mrs. Costello," she managed to croak from her bed, "where was that picture kept before you brought it in here?"

" 'Twas thrown aside with a lot of lumber down in the old gun room. Herself must have banished it there years ago when she put things belonging to Miss Sheila out of her sight. Most of the other photographs she burned, but this one she must have kept because there was a value on it, and there it was hidden in the gun room ever since—a place nobody uses, only Mr. Randy an odd time when he does be cleaning his guns. 'Twas only the search for the will took me there yesterday, and I saw the old picture and brought it up here. . . ."

Cathleen closed her eyes and listened no more. Had she really hoped to prove to herself that, after all, perhaps, Randy had never seen this telltale painting that so gave her away? Oh, it was silly, worse than silly, to let hope keep struggling through to be trying even now when her head ached fiercely, to find some excuse for dismissing last night's misery as so much imagination. It had not been imagination . . . just clear logical common sense coming to her rescue, saving her from the dreadful betrayal of that equivocal kiss.

And when presently out of the timeless confusion of this endless morning Randy himself was in her room, standing at the foot of her bed, gazing at her with grave concern in his gray eyes, she could only turn aside and hide her face in the pillows, begging him to go away.

"It is all my fault," he reproached himself, "letting you swim so far, leaving you on the island to catch your death of cold!"

"I'm all right," she told him almost angrily, "please go away. I'll be better tomorrow . . . I'm going home then. I've got to go home." The words rose in a wail of childish despair for she was too tired, too confused for subtleties.

"But Cathleen . . . you can't go home, my dear. You're far too ill!" The gently spoken reasonable words stabbed her. My dear! How could he keep up this ghastly pretense of affection? Tears burned her aching eyes.

"But I must go," she sobbed. "I cannot be ill here . . . I wish I had never come to this place!" A dreadful trapped sensation came to her then, a feeling that she would never get away from Castle Osborne, and she had to fight herself sternly, thrusting back the waves of sheer panic that threatened her. It was as though the walls of the room were closing in on her; suffocating, inimical, and Randy's face seemed to advance and recede like a face seen on the screen of a cinema—distorted, out of focus, terrifying. "Please go away! Please!" she cried brokenly, and saw the hurt, puzzled look in his eyes as he turned and tiptoed out of the room.

Left alone she was a little ashamed of her outburst, but she was too tired to care very much, and almost before the sound of his footsteps had died away she had fallen into a feverish doze. When she opened her eyes again Mollie was coming into the room carrying Yo-Yo wrapped up in a red blanket; his dark little monkey face peering mournfully through the folds.

"I thought I'd bring Yo-Yo to cheer you up," the child announced. "It's far too noisy for him in the kitchen and I'm sure his head aches. If you wouldn't mind having him at the foot of your bed . . . ."

After that everything seemed to become more natural and less frightening. Having Yo-Yo was comforting, for he soon tired of lying at the foot of the bed, and crept with hoarse purrs into the crook of Cathleen's arm. And when Mollie returned a little later with a good-looking cheery young doctor who prescribed for both human and animal invalids with delightful inconsequence, there was much heartening nonsense and laughter in which Cathleen found herself joining.

"It is no more than a severe chill you have—with the smallest touch of congestion there in the bronchial tubes," the doctor pronounced assuringly, in his lilting brogue. And Yo-Yo it seemed was much in the same state. "Let the two of you stay here in the warm room with a good fire for a couple of days and you will be as right as rain."

He would send up a fever mixture for the young lady, the doctor promised, and a few pills for the little cat.

"Isn't he divine!" Mollie sighed in schoolgirl devotion when he had gone. "I simply adore Dr. Mac, and he always helps me with my pets. Randy's old horse vet is no use at all with small animals. Once, when I rescued a swan off the lough that had a broken wing, Dr. Mac came all the way out from Dunbarragh and set it for me...."

Cathleen couldn't help finding this story singularly appealing. But Irish people were like that ... human, warm, utterly disarming. Even the sinister ones! There was Mrs. Costello transformed into a devoted nurse all at once! Through the three days of her illness Cathleen couldn't have had better care. And it wasn't only Mrs. Costello, the whole household seemed to conspire for her welfare; old Danny the gardener sending fruit and flowers every morning to the sickroom, the cook unseen in her kitchen racking her brains for special dishes to tempt an ailing appetite. They were all so kind; Randy driving the twenty miles into Dunbarragh to get ice for her sore throat, sending her up books and magazines by Mollie. He did not repeat his visit to her room, for which Cathleen was thankful.

So that she did not see him again until the first day of her convalescence, when she went rather shakily downstairs to sit by the fire that had been lighted for her special benefit in the library. Out of doors, the weather had broken and rain poured softly from a mild gray windless sky. Lying back in one of the deep, shabby leather armchairs Cathleen watched the small gold flames lick around the brown hairy sods of peat piled on the hearth, warning Yo-Yo who shared her interest in them, that flames were not moving objects suitable for a kitten to play with!

Fragile after her three days' illness, her skin held the warm pallor of magnolia blossom, her dark-lashed eyes a richer blue because of the faint shadows that encircled them. The lines of her face, too, sharpened by fever, emphasized the beauty of a bone structure almost classical in its perfection. Something of childish roundness had gone, she looked older, sadder, but never had she been lovelier. And though quite unaware of this, she had, with a sense of drama put on her prettiest day dress; a dove-gray clinging jersey cloth, to which for warmth she had added a coral pink cardigan. There were coral beads at her throat, and coral lipstick outlined the soft, firm young mouth.

This afternoon—if Randy came to her—she was determined to have things out with him. At least she could hint at her identity and watch his reaction. And she would tell him that her visit to Castle Osborne must end at once. Just why it had been necessary to take special pains with her appearance for this conversation she would not let herself inquire. Nor would she admit just how painful was the leap of her heart when presently the library door opened softly. But it was only Mollie carrying a heavy tea tray that she put on a small table beside the fire.

"You look like a flower," the little girl said, "one of those pale creamy roses with pinky centers. What a super dress!" Wistfully she fingered the fine clinging stuff. "You look like Yo-Yo, too," she added with a chuckle. "Dove-gray body and dark head and very blue eyes!"

As long as I don't look like the oil painting hidden in the wardrobe upstairs, Cathleen thought sadly. Somehow she was sure that whatever suspicions of her identity were afloat in the old house, Mollie had not shared in them. That was what made it such a relief to be in the child's cheery innocent company. If she had had any inkling of the complications in the air she would have blurted out something revealing long ago, she invariably said everything that came into her head. So that there was no need now for the quick pang of resentment when she announced, "Randy is tearing himself away from the Doon Hill bog where he is superintending the carting of the winter peat because you have come down to tea. He's dying to see you!"

The quick foolish color occasioned by this naive remark had hardly faded from Cathleen's cheeks when Randy himself appeared, the fine drops of rain still clinging to his dark hair, his old tweeds steaming and dark with dampness.

Holding her hand in greeting he looked down at her, and she could see the disconcerting flash of warmth that lit his gray eyes—as though he were really glad to see her. "You look wonderful!" he told her, and there was obvious relief in his tone. "What I've been through the last few days cursing myself for letting you in for the awful chill you caught . . . feeling like a murderer!"

The word made her shiver with the recollection of her dark thoughts during the onset of her fever. Randy wasn't a murderer—only a scheming, rather cold-blooded young man with an obsessive passion for Castle Osborne. And yet looking at him lounging comfortably and amiably in the old armchair at the other side of the hearth it was difficult to fit him into this picture. He was talking about the peat carting, saying that whoever was in Castle Osborne for the coming winter would be glad of the good stacks they were building in the empty stables.

"Probably you will be here yourself," Cathleen said, not able to meet his eyes as she offered this tentative bait. He shook his head. "Not very likely, I'm afraid. I phoned Philligan yesterday when I was in Dunbarragh, and it seems the chase for the missing Sheila is growing hot. At all events he has come across someone in Dublin who had heard that she lived in

London after Costello's death and married some doctor fellow there, and that they had a child.''

Cathleen's heart felt as though it had stopped forever as she put up a trembling hand to shield her eyes, and so loudly did the blood beat in her ears that she could hardly hear Randy as he went on to say that Philligan's informant hadn't been able to remember the name of the doctor Sheila Costello had married. Only that he lived somewhere in London . . . and there was one child. ''Poor Sheila died, it seems, soon after her second marriage,'' Randy continued. ''But that still leaves the child— who is obviously the person to inherit the FitzOsborne estate. Philligan has gone over to London to see what he can uncover in the birth and marriage records at Somerset House. It ought not to be hard now to get the whole thing cleared up.''

''And if the child turns out to be a girl,'' Mollie put in with the air of one determined to make the best of a bad job, ''it won't be so awful because Randy can marry her. We've already worked it all out. . . .''

''You even have a theme song about it,'' Cathleen murmured in a stifled voice.

She was aware of the horror in Randy's eyes as he stared at her. ''What on earth are you talking about?'' he demanded sharply.

For answer Cathleen began to hum softly the tune of the cynical song about the landless young man who schemed to marry a colleen for her gold.

A slow dark flush spread over Randy's face as he listened. ''You really think Mollie was serious just now . . . you think *that* of me!'' he asked with awful quietness, when she had finished.

''What else is there to think?'' Cathleen burst out bitterly. ''Why don't you stop pretending about everything . . . admit that you've known all along who I am!''

It was though a sudden deathly chill flowed into the firelit library then, as in utter and horrified silence the two young Kilmorans stared at their guest.

What have I done, oh, what have I done, cried Cathleen's heart in swift illogical panic—for she had done no more than speak her mind as she had planned. Only that in this silence that met her assault some quality unbargained for appeared. No guilt looked out at her from Randy's deep gray eyes, but the incredulous pain of a spirit mortally wounded.

And it was while the silence still held them there—three figures of stone—that the door of the library opened and Mrs. Costello's gray head was thrust in. "The clerk from Mr. Philligan's office is at the door, Mr. Randy. Will you see him in here?" she asked. But, before Randy had time to stir himself out of his trance to make a reply, a young man with thick red hair and a freckled face was coming into the room.

"Mr. Philligan told me to come up to you without delay, Mr. Kilmoran," he began in a nervous rush. "There's a long telegram from him. He said I was to break it to you gently that the matter of the FitzOsborne next of kin has been settled beyond all doubt, and that unless the missing will is produced, he's afraid you've lost all claim to Castle Osborne."

CHAPTER EIGHT

FOR A MOMENT there was a dreadful pause, then Randy said dryly, "You have a wonderful notion of breaking bad news gently, Mr. Rafferty! Sit down now and tell us the rest. Philligan has found Sheila FitzOsborne's child, I suppose?"

Young Mr. Rafferty lowered himself into a convenient chair, giving Cathleen an uneasy glance. "I didn't notice you had a visitor, Mr. Kilmoran," he began in stumbling apology.

Cathleen stood up on shaking legs. Things were happening too quickly now. Weak and shaken after her days of fever, she shrank from the implications of this new turn of events, even while recognizing that her own impetuous words just now had already precipitated the inevitable crisis. Whatever Mr. Philligan had discovered could only clear the air, settling any lingering doubt Randy and old Mrs. Costello may have had of the evidence of their senses. The girl who looked like Sheila FitzOsborne's daughter *was* Sheila FitzOsborne's daughter. But to the uninitiated Mr. Rafferty she was still a stranger. His words had invited her withdrawal from a family conference, and indeed she would be glad enough to withdraw. But as she turned toward the door she heard Randy say quietly, "Hadn't you better stay and hear this out?"

Limply she sank back into the leather armchair once more, aware of the disconcerted glance the solicitor's clerk gave her as he took a crumpled envelope from his pocket.

"I have Mr. Philligan's telegram here with me," he said, handing a sheaf of small pages to Randy, who read them through in silence. It seemed an unbearable time before he raised his dark head and turned to Mollie, who was kneeling on the hearth rug looking very young and scared. "What does it say, Randy?" the child whispered.

Randy was ashen gray now and the thrust of his chin was grim. In the short space of time during which he had pondered the telegram his face seemed to have changed beyond recognition. Either Philligan's communication, in spite of Cathleen's attempt to forestall it, came to him as an overwhelming surprise, or he was a consummate actor. He looked dazed and bewildered . . . and coldly angry.

He said, "Sheila Costello married a London doctor in 1927. A daughter was born to them in 1928 and at the same time Sheila died. . . ."

"The daughter is grown up then," Mollie put in, with a naive eagerness that might have indicated that she had not forgotten their desperate plan for a marriage of convenience!

"She is almost twenty-one," Randy said. "Philligan says he hasn't been able to contact her yet because the house she lives in was closed up when he called there; the family being away at the seaside for their summer holiday."

"But he's going down to Bognor, the wire says," Mr. Rafferty prompted. "He'll have met her by this time I expect. I wonder what sort of a young girl is she? Maybe she'd be amenable to some kind of compromise. After all, the whole countryside is ready to give evidence that it was Lady FitzOsborne's wish to leave the estate to yourself, Mr. Randy, and that there was a will to that effect. If it came to a court case there's no judge but would have sympathy for you. There is such a thing as the principle of equity in the legal system of this country, don't forget!"

Randy looked across at Cathleen sitting frozen and huddled in the deep armchair. It was a look of pure and concentrated scorn. "I don't think we'll ask her to trouble about compromises," he said. So venomously and deliberately were these words directed at her, and so clearly had Randy prolonged the oblique conversation with Mollie and Rafferty for her discomfort, that Cathleen's spirit revolted. "Doesn't Mr. Philligan give you the name of Sheila FitzOsborne's second husband . . . the name of her daughter?" she asked sharply.

"Yes," Randy returned with maddening brevity, "He does."

"Then why don't you tell Mollie?"

"*You* tell her," Randy said.

Cathleen drew in a quick, anguished breath. It was as though they were alone in the room now, their eyes meeting in hot bright anger.

"Something you might have told us both more honorably a fortnight ago," Randy went on in a low voice. "Why didn't you tell us?"

"Why should I have told you something you already knew?" Cathleen countered doggedly.

Randy passed a hand slowly across his furrowed brow. He looked suddenly almost sick with bewilderment. "But how could I have known?" he asked wearily.

"Mrs. Costello knows. Anyone who has seen that oil painting you kept in the gun room couldn't fail to have recognized me. . . ."

Randy stared at her with such honest blankness, that the first awful touch of misgiving made itself felt.

"I haven't a notion what you are talking about," he said. "What painting in the gun room? I didn't know there were any paintings there. My great-aunt used a part of the gun room to store litter in . . . boxes of moth-eaten furs, broken furniture and derelict ornaments. If there were canvases mixed up with the rest of the junk I never saw them . . . and, anyway, what can a painting have to do with . . . the matter in hand?"

"A picture of Sheila FitzOsborne at the age of eighteen,"

Cathleen brought out in a stifled tone. "If you'd ever seen it . . . ."

Randy shook his head. "But I didn't," he said, and Cathleen felt the blood drain from her heart, for suddenly, abjectly she knew that he spoke the truth. And with his denial her whole case against him seemed to collapse. The revelations leaping upon him one after another this afternoon had been revelations indeed, stark and cruel in their unexpectedness. The very vibrations of the room seemed filled now with the pain of his honest astonishment. All too clearly she recalled the absence of guilt with which he had met her first monstrous hint of his duplicity. Not cunning unmasked, but a mortal wound had looked at her out of his wondering gray eyes, when just before Rafferty's entry she had flung at him her accusing, "Why don't you admit that you have known all along who I am?" And now as those truthful eyes watched her, still wondering, still filled with that incalculable pain, the room swam around her.

What have I done to him, she asked herself once more. *Oh, what have I done?*

"The young lady's name is Trenton," announced Mr. Rafferty, who had apparently grown tired of the mysterious and irrelevant exchange going on between Mr. Kilmoran and his visitor. "Cathleen Trenton . . . the doctor Sheila married, you see, was Trenton. . . ."

Cathleen heard Mollie's little spurt of laughter. "But it can't be Trenton," the child said. "Cathleen Trenton is *here*." Her small brown hand waved wildly, *"This* is Cathleen Trenton," she said, indicating the huddled figure in the big armchair.

Mr. Rafferty took the announcement calmly. "Only that this Cathleen is spelled with a *C* in the Gaelic way," he said. "And she lives in a London suburb called Petunia Road."

Cathleen leaned forward out of her chair. "I am Cathleen Trenton of Petunia Road, Mr. Rafferty," she said slowly. "My mother was Sheila FitzOsborne."

The freckled face went wooden with shock. It could have been funny if the whole thing had not been so tragic to see the untidy red head turn this way and that as the young clerk stared first at Cathleen then at Randy. "B-but," he spluttered, "I don't get it. I don't get it at all. If Miss Trenton had already arrived here, why didn't ye recall Mr. Philligan?"

"Why indeed!" murmured Randy wretchedly. "There are a lot of things about this sickening muddle to be cleared up. I'm as much at sea as you are, Rafferty...."

Cathleen straightened her slim shoulders and her pale face took on a look of grim resolution. She was aware of the three pairs of eyes watching her . . . waiting for her to speak, and for one desperate moment she tried to collect her scattered thoughts. What she said now was going to be all-important. If she could only make Randy understand . . . see just how the whole horrible slippery set of circumstances had ensnared her! If she could only undo even a fraction of the harm she had brought to their blossoming friendship! Suddenly, unnervingly, the memory of the night on the lough returned to her . . . Randy's arms around her as they stood by the hydrangea bush . . . Randy's kiss. And his wistful apology afterward: "This is no time to go falling in love . . . me without a penny to my name, no job, no home probably. Only that love doesn't wait for things like that!"

Tears thickened her throat as she began her stumbling explanation; the sheer innocence with which she had come to this place, her incredulous terror on the night she had found herself confronted by a grandmother she had never wished to meet. She had chosen Osbornestown for her holiday because she had believed the FitzOsbornes long gone from the district and there had been nothing but a natural curiosity to see her mother's native place.

"Then you know how it was." Her blue eyes sought Randy's set young face in wistful pleading. "Talking to you in the train because of Yo-Yo, Mrs. Callaghan not having room for me, and your kindness in asking me here. . . .''

"You mean you've been here ever since before Lady FitzOsborne died!" Mr. Rafferty put in with horror, but none of them took any notice of him.

"But when grandam died," Mollie prompted, "when we talked about the will and everything in front of you . . . why didn't you say something then?"

"I thought . . . I felt I had no right," Cathleen answered stumblingly. "I was frightened by the whole extraordinary affair. I couldn't take it in that I was really the heiress to this great place . . . or that you would believe me if I said I was Sheila's daughter. I kept on hoping, too, the missing will would turn up. . . .''

"Why?" Randy shot at her.

"Because Lady FitzOsborne hated my mother . . . would have hated me, too, if she had known me. And she wanted you to have Castle Osborne. . . .''

"There you are," Mr. Rafferty interrupted again in a great hurry. "Miss Trenton has the rights of it. There could be some adjustment, I'm certain. . . .'' Again none of them noticed him.

"I just . . . wanted to go home, escape from the whole incredible muddle," Cathleen was saying wearily, "and first I stayed on because Mollie asked me to help her through the funeral . . . then because I caught this chill. . . .''

Randy's face darkened as though he were remembering too sharply the reason for the chill. He said, "And all the time you were thinking we knew who you were . . . that's the part of it that seems to be so unaccountable . . . so crazy. . . .''

"I didn't think it all the time," Cathleen faltered. "I had an uneasy feeling that Mrs. Costello suspected my identity, but I wasn't sure until she produced that picture of my mother. It is so exactly like me that I knew she had hung it in my room to confound me."

"With my collaboration," Randy said. Turning from the burning anger in his eyes she knew that her floundering explanation had failed, that it had been the wildest optimism to hope it could do otherwise. Apologies, further explanations . . . they could do no good. Everything she said would only incriminate her more and more. Her brain reeled as she sought for words that still might ease a little her desperate plight . . . and Randy's. For he had loved her . . . she could see it now in anguished retrospect. Reserved, self-contained, too absorbed in his schemes for the reclaiming of the lost lands of Castle Osborne to have had time in his life for tenderness, he had found in her some quality that had pierced his preoccupation, made him aware of her. He had let his armor slip, grown vulnerable . . . perhaps in a mildly sentimental fashion only. But there had been at least the beginning of love in his gentleness for her, his desire to have her near him.

Color flooded her pale cheeks, tears trembled on the thick dark lashes. "Randy," she began wildly, all coherence deserting her, "it isn't quite the way you think it is . . . if I could talk to you . . . alone. . . ."

He looked at her coldly. "Your interest in the selling of the garden produce," he said, "your concern for the empty pastures! And I was so impressed by your thrift, your sympathy! It's very funny really." His laughter was bitter to hear, killing her last hope of reconciliation. With death in her heart, she saw him turn to the bemused-looking Rafferty. "This is all very confusing for you, Rafferty," he said. "But it is confusing for me, too. Just why Miss Trenton chose to stay in this house for the past fortnight without disclosing her relationship to the FitzOsborne family, you have perhaps been able to gather from her explanation . . . just why she allowed us to incur the expense of the search carried out by private inquiry agent; why Mr. Philligan was permitted to go to Dublin first and then to London spending a great deal of money in the process; all this you may be able to understand with your clear legal mind. I confess it baffles me utterly.''

He stood up, tall, rigid, formidable, and for one awful moment Cathleen thought he was going to walk out of the room . . . out of the house . . . out of her life then and there. But it was only to the hearth he went, groping in the pipe stand on the great mantelshelf for a pipe that he began to fill. Relief, ridiculous, out of all proportion, flooded her overwrought heart, at the sight of this homely action. And young Rafferty rubbing his red head, was grinning at her, saying, ''Indeed then, it would take more than the clearest legal mind on earth to understand the ways of a woman. Only that I'm sure Miss Trenton meant no harm. . . . Hadn't she everything to gain by shouting out to the world who she was . . . and she didn't shout, only keeping it all to herself, worrying herself sick thinking the heritage by rights belonged to the man the dead poor lady willed it to.''

As long as she lived Cathleen felt, she would be grateful to this unknown but imaginative young Irishman, who could be generously if somewhat ambiguously construe her motives!

''What we have to do now,'' he went on, ''is to wire and tell Mr. Philligan he can stop gallivanting around the south coast of England and come home. After that . . . we'll see. There's a power of formalities to be gone through before the transfer of any inheritance can be made final.''

''There needn't be any formalities,'' Cathleen said in a small voice. ''I don't want Castle Osborne.'' Tears hung on her dark lashes. She felt sick and weak and her heart was a lump of ice that would never melt again. She had hurt Randy in the most horrible way, and as long as he lived he would hate her . . . if he ever thought about her at all. Nothing would ever come right about this nightmare inheritance now. She had spoiled the wonderful chance of a solution that fate had held almost within her grasp . . . almost. If Randy had known her identity earlier there would have been no tender interlude. Fiercely independent and proud he would have died rather than use their love to solve this tangle of wills and property deeds. She knew that now. So that whatever course she had taken, she would have lost him. There was only one small gleam of comfort left in the fact that she could still refuse to supplant him in his heritage.

"I just want to go home to Petunia Road and forget I ever heard of Castle Osborne," she said with a stifled sob.

"I'm afraid it's not so simple as that," Mr. Rafferty reminded her, his freckled face puckered with stupefaction. People didn't usually weep when they found themselves within reach of a slice of luck like the inheritance of a large estate! "It would be very awkward for us to have you away in London just now," he went on. "I must ask you to remain at least until Mr. Philligan gets back to advise you. I couldn't take the responsibility of accepting any snap decisions you might feel inclined to make at this stage."

"I *can't* stay here," Cathleen began wretchedly, and suddenly her head went down into her hands.

"If anyone leaves this house, I do!" she heard Randy declare grimly, and Mr. Rafferty answering that there was no need for either of the claimants to rush from the scene. "Things can be adjusted," the young man went on doggedly. "Of that I'm certain. Miss Trenton is taking a more than reasonable view of the whole situation, and in any case until the will, or absence of a will, has been proved the estate is a kind of no man's land. You've been acting as Lady FitzOsborne's bailiff for two years, Mr. Randy, and she gave you a power of attorney that still holds good. The sensible thing for you to do is to carry on here with the harvesting of the crops and the upkeep of the place generally. It may be weeks before we've got the legal side of things worked out."

There was a miserable silence while Cathleen fought back the waves of hysterical exhaustion that threatened her. She didn't want to cry here in front of the cold-eyed Randy and puzzled Mr. Rafferty, but her heart was bursting with its grief, and, weak from her days of fever, control was difficult. Raising her drenched blue eyes she forced herself to say shakily, "I've got to be in London by the end of the month, anyhow. I've a job to go back to . . . the office in which I work. . . ."

She was aware suddenly of Mollie watching her, the green eyes wide with awe. "Poor Cathleen!" the child whispered, and suddenly she was kneeling by the leather armchair, her hand on Cathleen's arm, her young face warm with pity. "Don't be so unhappy about everything, please!" she begged. "We aren't angry with you. You can't help being Sheila's daughter, and it is very easy to understand how hard it was for you to tell us about it. We knew during the last day or two that Mr. Philligan was going to produce *somebody* to disinherit Randy . . . and as long as it had to be that way, we'd much rather it was you than anyone else. Wouldn't we, Randy?" She turned to her brother who regarded her stonily, making no reply.

"I don't really see why he has got to be so nasty about it," she said a moment later when he had gone to see Mr. Rafferty out of the house.

Cathleen looked at her with hollow eyes. "There are things in this muddle Randy will never forgive me for . . . never as long as he lives, because they are unforgivable," she said in a dead dry voice. With a shiver then she stood up, drawing the coral cardigan close for warmth. "I'm going back to bed—and I think I'd better stay there until Mr. Philligan returns!" she said, ending with a tremulous little laugh.

"No you won't," Mollie declared stoutly. "You'll rest tonight, and tomorrow you'll be feeling much better about everything. We'll go out picnicking on the lough if it is fine and Randy will get over his tantrums and remember how much he likes you. Maybe you'll both fall in love with each other in the end . . . just as I've hoped you would ever since you came here...long before I knew you were a FitzOsborne. It has been so lovely having you...just as though you were one of the family; which of course, you are now!'' The green eyes flashed mischievously. ''It wouldn't be the first time a FitzOsborne married a Kilmoran,'' the unquenchable child said softly.

''Don't!'' Cathleen cried in sharp anguish. ''Please, Mollie, don't say things like that ever again!''

But Mollie's sweetness and friendliness were very comforting in the strange and difficult days that followed. Ingenuous, irrepressible, she insisted upon regarding the revelation of Cathleen's identity as the greatest blessing that could have befallen them in the circumstances. ''Think, if it had been some awful grasping female who would have wanted to turn us out right away!'' she would bring out in the middle of one of the strained and agonizing mealtimes, when Randy and Cathleen faced each other in silence across the Chippendale table.

Now when he spoke to her at all it was about the affairs of the estate, deferring to her with an icy punctiliousness as though she were already the owner of the broad, wild lands. And in spite of herself, in spite of the quiet misery going on all the time in her heart, she couldn't help being interested in the problems he presented to her. It was the day after Mr. Rafferty's visit that he talked to her about the reclaimed meadow—his pet project. ''It is Italian rye grass and clover mixed we have put down,'' he told her as gravely as though she had been an experienced farmer. ''And it ought not to be allowed to get as far as seeding. We could have it cut, of course, but if it is mown for hay it dies out very quickly and all my work on that particular patch will have been wasted.''

''You mean it ought to have cattle eating it before the seeds fall?'' she asked.

''It ought to be grazed,'' he agreed. ''And there aren't any substantial farmers near enough to make it easy to let out.''

She knew he was thinking of his Herefords. Well, if Herefords would comfort him . . . !

"How many cows would you want and how much would they cost?" she inquired.

"Bullocks," he corrected patiently. "We could do with a dozen to begin with. The bank might advance the sum needed, and the biggest cattle fair of the year takes place at Dunbarragh on Friday."

"Well!" She gave him her long serious look. "It seems pretty obvious what we ought to do, doesn't it?"

"It's up to you," he countered stiffly.

She drew in a long quivering breath. "Randy . . . it's not up to me. It's *your* land. As soon as Mr. Philligan gets back he'll . . . fix everything so that there isn't any question about your ownership."

She saw a tremor that might have been impatience . . . or something much deeper, cross his somber handsome face. "Mr. Philligan can't fix anything of the kind," he said. "It would take I imagine at least a court injunction."

He gave her that oddly impatient look again. "You feel like this only because you're scared over the rather muddling way you got into all this," he said. "If you'd never heard of Castle Osborne . . . hadn't come here and got mixed up with our end of the story, if you'd been sitting in Petunia Road with Mr. Philligan dropping out of the sky to tell you you were an heiress, it would be a very different story."

"Of course it would."

"Well then! You're being illogical . . . taking a superficial view of the whole thing. Deep down you're as keen on owning this place as I am; you've got the Irish landlust in you . . . like all Kilmorans."

"Kilmorans?" she ecoed, the color running up into her cheeks.

"Your grandmother was a Kilmoran," he reminded her.

Just hearing him say it brought that swift surge of emotion she'd been experiencing at intervals ever since she came to Castle Osborne . . . that hot, possessive love, the yearning pride that came to her at the very sight of the gray stones of the old house and the wide boundaries of the rolling lands. And now to have Randy acknowledge her as a Kilmoran seemed to loosen this strange passion within her, opening doors in her heart she had been too timid to open herself. "How do you know the way I feel?" she challenged him, her blue eyes blazing.

"I just do know," he said quietly.

Because we are the same blood, she thought, and the wild-rose color flooded her cheeks. "As long as you don't go away from here . . ." she found herself bargaining impetuously, "I won't go, either."

He said, "I won't go unless I have to for very definite legal reasons. This isn't a matter for childish pique."

"No, indeed," she agreed earnestly, "it's a matter for intelligent and grown-up compromise. I could never be happy here if I felt I had dispossessed you . . . and Mollie. There must be some way we can arrange it all."

But he didn't answer that, and it seemed to her that the scorn was there in his gray eyes again as he turned away from her. "I'll go into Dunbarragh and arrange with the bank for a loan for Friday's cattle fair," he said.

Perhaps he would invite her to go to the castle fair with him! Or, if he did not suggest it himself, she could easily, in her new and powerful position, maneuver him into taking her. After all, the Herefords were as much her concern now as his. This breathtaking thought carried her through the next three days on a wave of secret excitement and still more secret hope. After all, if she and Randy went around together, sharing such vital interests as Herefords and cattle fairs, running the estate on this basis of quiet mutual discussion, might not the barrier between them gradually be overcome? And at least it was faintly comforting just to be with Randy, watching him, listening to him, learning something of his skill with this land they both loved—the crumbs upon which she must now feed her hungry heart!

But in the end Cathleen did not go to the Friday cattle fair . . . for it was on Thursday evening Mr. Philligan came home. He did not come alone. He brought Len Cranton with him . . . a Len dispatched by Mrs. Trenton with the urgent messages of counsel she could not dispense in person, because it was impossible for her to leave the children—Petunia Road's reaction to an Irish solicitor's astounding announcement! It was Len, the only male available, who must convey family congratulations, family advice.

Coming up from the lough shores where she had been picnicking with Mollie and Yo-Yo, Cathleen saw the solicitor's familiar white raincoat emerge from a mud-spattered car, and seeing then another equally familiar overcoat emerge she stood still in her tracks, her heart dying within her.

CHAPTER NINE

IF ONLY RANDY hadn't been there on the terrace! He didn't usually come in from the farm at this hour, and today they were busy cutting oats on the high pastures of Doon while a brief spell of fine weather held. What unlucky chance had brought him away from the harvesting just at this awkward moment? Dreading the prospect of meeting Len under his keen and disconcerting scrutiny, Cathleen dragged herself up the incline that led through the flowering hydrangeas. Never did she pass this spot now without remembering the night of their swimming adventure, that hot swift kiss that had seemed to her the ultimate betrayal!

Mollie said, "Oh, heck! There's Philligan. What a bore! Now everything will be stirred up again and we were all getting on so peaceably. Why does there have to be so much talk about wills and property and who owns what? If they'd just let us drift on the way we've been doing the past three days how much easier it would be!"

Cathleen nodded in absent agreement. The arrival of Philligan could only mean fresh trouble, but anything Philligan could say was as nothing to the catastrophe of Len Cranton's appearance. How could her stepmother have been so tactless as to have sent him? But Mrs. Trenton had always liked Len, discussing family affairs with him, treating him as though he were already engaged to Cathleen. She might have guessed something of the kind would happen! Cathleen thought as she drew nearer to the group by the great hall door. How slight and town-bred—in spite of his Bognor tan—Len seemed beside the massive Randy!

She had reached the foot of the moss-grown steps now and saw Len turn to her, his shy, boyish face alight. "Cath! Gosh, it's good to see you!" She had to take the two hands he held out to her, and for one hideous moment wondered if he were going to kiss her! But he contented himself with a long hungering look that swept her from head to foot. "Your mom is in a bit of a flap over all this news of the inheritance," he was explaining then. "Wanted to come to you herself . . . but she couldn't get away with the move back from Bognor on her hands. So she asked me to pop over . . . ."

"There wasn't the slightest need for anyone to come," Cathleen couldn't stop herself saying, and hoped it didn't sound too unfriendly. She was horribly aware of Randy watching them, a puzzled frown on his brow. And Philligan, too, holding back as though her moment with Len Cranton was something too intimate for his intrusion. Feeling awkward and wretched she stood there her hands imprisoned in Len's.

"I'm under strict instructions to bring you back with me," he was telling her emphatically. "Your mom says it's high time you gave up all this wild adventuring and came back to the fold."

Cathleen stared at him in horror. Somehow hearing him speak so calmly of her return to Petunia Road made her realize afresh how utterly established she felt at Castle Osborne.

Mr. Philligan was surging forward then, booming in his hearty way. "Well! Well! So this is the little lady who has given us all such a run for our money . . . or rather *her* money!"

Looking over his shoulder Cathleen could see Lanty Conor a little way along the terrace moving deck chairs, fidgeting with the small folding table on which they sometimes had tea . . . quite obviously, and without any subtlety, eavesdropping. Nobody ever bothered to take the deck chairs in at night; if it rained they got wet. Lanty's sudden solicitude for them was just comical.

"Hadn't we better go indoors," Cathleen suggested. "You will want tea or a drink of some kind . . . after your long journey. Did you drive from Dublin?" Leading the way in then—just as though it were her own house—her crazy beautiful castle!

With the corner of her eye she was aware of Randy slipping away down the steps, dark-faced, somber, his mouth set in grim lines.

"Please, don't go!" she called to him. "We can't talk things over without you. You've got to be in on this."

"He certainly has!" agreed Philligan. "Come on, Kilmoran. Open up a bottle now and tell me just what was the meaning of that extraordinary telegram I got from you?"

They were in the great shabby library then; Len in his dark city overcoat standing awed and quiet staring at the high book-lined walls, the cavernous hearth with its carved mantel, the long narrow windows framing lough water and pansy-blue hills. But they were all a little tongue-tied suddenly, like actors groping for forgotten lines.

"Do sit down," Cathleen urged at last, ending this interval of awkward hesitancy. "If we could have some drinks . . ." she said, turning to Randy. If he wouldn't play host then she must offer the hospitality of the castle. But she felt nervous doing it, like an interloper. If he would only look at her, speak to her, or at least say something welcoming to Len!

"Fine old place you've got here!" Len was murmuring in his banal way as he lowered himself uninvited into a vast armchair.

"And every stone of it likely to become the property of one, Miss Cathleen Trenton!" boomed Philligan. He grinned across at Cathleen. "Now perhaps you'll tell us just why you decided to visit Castle Osborne just at this juncture, Miss Trenton, and why, having got here, you didn't make yourself known?"

With a small resigned sigh Cathleen embarked on the

explanation she had already given to Mr. Rafferty. And this time it went better. She wasn't so nervous. Nor did she make so much of her desire to withdraw all claim of inheritance. But she did say that she hoped they would be able to arrive at some friendly arrangement.

"Lady FitzOsborne wanted Mr. Kilmoran to have the estate," she emphasized. "I don't see why he should lose everything merely because of a missing piece of paper."

Randy, siphoning soda into the glasses of whiskey he had poured out, made an impatient sound. "Spare us the heroics, please!" he mocked. "I don't want any friendly arrangements, thank you! All I want is justice. If I've lost this place because of the missing will . . . then I've lost it. I'm quite ready to get out." The gray eyes flashed—the pupils gone crimson. How illogical he was! Imploringly Cathleen looked at him. Had he forgotten his sensible remark the other day about "childish pique."

"Now listen to me, the two of you!" Mellowed by whiskey Mr. Philligan beamed at them in a fatherly way. "This thing has to be handled slowly. No need for fireworks! No need at all. In ten days' time Miss Trenton will be twenty-one. Until that date Castle Osborne belongs, in fact, to no one. So that gives us ten more days to find the missing will—if it is to be found. And if not, ten perfectly good day in which some other solution to the whole thing may occur. In the meantime I suggest you just stay on here, Miss Trenton, as though you were still simply having your holiday. And you, Kilmoran, your best course is to do all in your power to find that will . . . that goes without saying. As I drew it up myself, I'm pretty sure of its existence; documents of that kind don't just walk away on their own!"

"Then where is it?" Randy asked quietly, all the fire gone out of him, his face blankly hopeless.

Philligan shrugged. "Maybe Mrs. Costello could enlighten us. After all, she's the one who had constant access to the sickroom where it was kept."

"And she is the one person in the world who wouldn't have destroyed it," Randy said. "She is pro-Kilmoran, if ever a woman was, and never ceases day or night searching for the will; in fact, she seems to have gone half-batty over its loss."

"Why?" the lawyer asked crisply.

"Because she hated my mother," Cathleen offered in a small voice. "And hated, too, FitzOsborne's husband. She hates all the FitzOsbornes, and has taken the trouble to tell me so. Lady FitzOsborne was a Kilmoran, don't forget, and all through her life it was her dream to get the Osborne property somehow into the hands of her own family. At least that's what Mrs. Costello says."

Philligan gave her a shrewd look. "You seem to have got a good deal out of the old girl!"

"She has been talking to me and at me since the day I arrived here," Cathleen said. "I think it is quite clear that she saw my resemblance to my mother from the very first." She couldn't bear to look at Randy as she made this observation with its awful echoes of their miserable conversation the day Mr. Rafferty had called.

She heard him move impatiently, jingling the tray of glasses and bottles on the table on which he had perched. But before he had time to make any comment, Len was leaning forward in his vast chair saying to Mr. Philligan, "This suggestion of yours that Miss Trenton should stay on here until her twenty-first birthday won't be very acceptable to her family. There's to be a big do for the occasion at her own home, a dance, presents, champagne . . . all that kind of thing. Her mother is making great preparations."

"My stepmother," Cathleen corrected, perhaps a little too meticulously. But the thought of Petunia Road and all the fuss for her birthday was suddenly too suffocating to be endured. And Philligan's declaration of the will's undoubted existence had shaken her. If it were, after all, to turn up, she would go back to her suburban home, her London office, and this Irish interlude would fade out as though it had never been. She would never see Randy again.

Odd, how seldom she allowed herself to face the thought that this culmination to the will situation was still a possibility! And odder still that in spite of her discomfort in the present atmosphere at the castle it would be all heaven to hear Mr. Philligan answer Len firmly that birthday party or no birthday party Miss Trenton's place was at Castle Osborne until some kind of decision about the property had been made. "It would be highly awkward for us to have her away in London when it comes to what we might call 'zero hour'," he said.

"But of course I must stay here," Cathleen agreed, glancing eagerly at Randy, who studiously avoided her eyes. And it was just at that moment the library door opened explosively to admit Mollie, her handkerchief to her mouth as she smothered her giggles. "That Lanty Conor!" she whispered conspiratorially.

"Would you believe it? There he was kneeling at the library door just now with his ear to the keyhole . . . just like someone in a funny play. You should have seen his face when I came along and caught him. He's gone scuttling off looking simply furious. Aren't servants the limit!"

"Well, he got a good earful for his trouble!" Randy said dryly. "It won't be long now before the whole story is all over the house."

"And all over the country," added Mr. Philligan grimly, "with Mrs. Costello saying, 'I told you so!' "

After that it was rather a dreadful evening. Len, who was due at his office on Monday, would return to England the following day. Tonight he would have to sleep at the castle and realizing this Cathleen offered him a bed—rather over Randy's head. Oh, it was awful, this awkward half owning Castle Osborne and not really owning it; and the way Randy refused to help in the smallest degree, pointedly ignoring Len's existence all through dinner. A ghastly meal with Lanty leering at them knowingly over a series of ill-cooked dishes . . . evidence of the chaos already reigning in a gossiping kitchen. Only Mr. Philligan's cheery presence saved the hour from utter disaster, and even he couldn't prevent Len saying things that made Cathleen's blood run cold. That moment of ultimate horror when he announced blithely in his thin polite Petunia Road voice, "Your mom thinks that if you do inherit this place, Cath, you ought to sell it outright. After all, what on earth could you do with a tumbledown Irish castle surrounded by rough hills and bogs . . . miles from civilization. . . ."

Cathleen could feel herself turning quite white. "But Len! My mother's home! I couldn't possibly sell it. You don't understand!"

She caught the flash of response in Randy's eyes. For one blissful instant they looked at one another, bound in that hot accord that could exclude all Petunia Road and its suburban standards—two Kilmorans defending their wild hills against the world!

In the lingering western twilight a little later she walked with Len up the long slope of Doon, a stroll he had himself bluntly demanded. "I've got to talk to you alone and there's so little time," he'd announced with a glance of open distaste for the group around the coffee cups. And almost as soon as they were out of the house he was saying he didn't like that fellow Randy.

"I don't trust him, Cath—the way he glowers at you . . . a bad-tempered Irishman who'd knife you in the back as soon as look at you! After all, it's to his advantage to get you out of the way. If you didn't exist he'd come into the property without any question—I got that out of Philligan on the way over from England. It's madness staying on in this house in such circumstances. And that crazy-looking bloke with the fair hair and wild blue eyes; listening at doors and watching you at dinnertime every moment of the time he was in the room. He's up to something, that fellow!''

She laughed at his fears. ''All Lanty is interested in is getting drunk as often as he can. And as for Randy . . . .'' But she couldn't discuss Randy seriously with Len Cranton. ''He may be a bit on edge just now, who wouldn't be?'' she admitted. ''But he is a man of honor . . . a gentleman.'' Her voice went soft as she remembered how utterly Randy had refused her quixotic offer to withdraw from the Castle Osborne inheritance—how clearly he had understood her love for the place. ''He's all right,'' she ended lamely. ''He's . . . good!''

She could feel Len studying her profile with sudden intentness. ''You aren't in love with him by any chance, are you?'' he asked with loverlike perception and a lover's quick jealousy.

''He's a . . . distant cousin,'' Cathleen answered evasively. ''We are both Kilmorans.'' Just saying it brought that swift thrill of pride! She turned to look back at the sweep of land behind them, the shadowy heather-clad hillside falling away to the lush valley of trees that held the proud old castle. Pale as a dream the great lough lay in its circle of darkening mountains. The milky sweetness of its vast waters breathed in the moist air that fanned her cheeks, and far beneath them, a bright banner of courage in the twilight, lay Randy's green field!

''You wouldn't understand the way I feel about . . . Randy Kilmoran . . . about everything here . . .'' she whispered. ''You *couldn't* understand.''

''No, I suppose not,'' Len agreed bitterly, ''I'm just the obscure bloke you grew up with . . . not to be compared with these grand titled relations you've unearthed!''

''Please don't talk like that, Len!'' She put an impulsive hand on his arm and instantly he had covered it with his own.

''You haven't changed then, Cath?''

''You know I haven't! We've always been good friends, Len.''

"Only that?"

"Isn't that enough?"

For answer he slid an arm around her shoulders. "Come home, Cath!" he pleaded. "Let that black-browed Irishman have his moth-eaten castle and forget about it. I don't want you to be an heiress . . . I want you the way you've always been. We could be so happy! My people are quite willing to have the top floor of our house made into a flat for us if we marry . . . until we could find a little place of our own." She could feel the slight shudder that ran through him as he looked out at the savage landscape. "What do you want with this godforsaken land?" he asked. "You'd die of loneliness here in your great castle. Think of it in winter time! Come home, Cath, darling, and let's announce our engagement on your twenty-first birthday."

"Len, dear, you know it's no good. We've had all this out so many times before. You're my friend . . . I like you so much . . . but I can't marry you. It's nothing to do with Castle Osborne— it's just—" her voice shook a little because she hated hurting him "—just that I don't love you in that way, Len!"

She could feel his lips come down lightly, softly on the curls at her brow. "Okay, sweet! I won't urge you any more just now. But I'm not giving up hope. Just tell me one thing. . . ." His arm tightened around her. "You're not staying on here because you're in love with that Randy fellow, are you?"

But before she had time to answer this question or free herself from Len's arms, there was Randy himself striding toward them over the springy grass that had deadened all sound of his approach. How much had he heard? Had he seen that tentative unwanted kiss, Cathleen wondered in misery. At least it was obvious that he had seen their significant attitude—a man and a woman in close embrace in the soft, sweet twilight. Moving apart from one another now with the hurried air of lovers surprised, they began to descend the path the tall figure was mounting.

"Nice evening for a walk," Randy murmured in banal greeting, as he passed them without slackening his pace. His face was wooden . . . utterly without expression of any kind. Only for an instant as he glanced at Cathleen there was that strange flash of ruby light in the dark centers of his eyes. He had a gun over his shoulder.

"Shooting!" Len muttered presently, with such stifled horror in his tone that Cathleen had to laugh in spite of herself.

"Just rabbits, I expect," she supplied. "This is the half-light in which all farmers like to go rabbit shooting."

"Is it?" Len murmured in town-bred incredulity. "As long as he keeps to rabbits, I don't mind! But they're all just a bit too handy with their trigger fingers, these Irish hotheads. . . ."

"Len, what utter rot. You don't know the first thing about the Irish . . . their heads aren't a bit hotter than yours. In fact, they are in a great many ways an exceedingly cool and logical people." She gave it up; it was hopeless trying to reason with Len in his present mood. All the way back to the castle she had to listen to him pleading endlessly and stubbornly that she should return to England with him the following day.

Her stepmother had been uneasy about her ever since she had heard of Joan Kent's defection. "We all hated the thought of you being stuck in this outlandish place alone," he urged, "and now that all this fuss about your Irish relations has cropped up, it is just more than I can bear to go back without you. Besides, you can't possibly be away from home for your birthday. You've no idea how hurt your mom will be. . . ."

Finally, for peace's sake she was forced to promise that whatever cropped up about the will and her inheritance, she would return to Petunia Road the day after her birthday. She'd have to go back sometime, she argued with herself inwardly, if only to collect her personal belongings and disentangle herself from her job at Gilmer & Co.

''We'll have the twenty-first birthday party a day late then,'' Len agreed, and had to be content with that.

He left the next morning soon after dawn, driving to Dunbarragh with Randy who was off to the cattle fair. Lying in her vast four-poster bed Cathleen heard them go rattling away through the quiet morning, her eyes filling with tears as she remembered how eagerly she had hoped she might have been asked to help with the buying of the Herefords. But all her poor little dreams of a gradual reconciliation between herself and Randy seemed quite empty and foolish now. Philligan's explosive return, the arrival of Len with his possessive air . . . that kiss in the twilight . . . oh, it was all so hopeless! Restlessly she turned on her pillows. She could almost hear Len's voice running on as he sat by Randy's side. He would never be able to keep silent while they covered that long twenty miles. He would talk of Petunia Road and of his years of friendship with the girl he had come so far now to see. He would hint at his hopes . . . perhaps do much more than hint, tactically warning the Irishman not to poach on his preserves. Len was a grim and relentless fighter in his own dogged English way, and he had been so instantly jealous of Randy. Which, of course, was quite fatuous. It hadn't taken her discovery of Randy Kilmoran to make Cathleen realize that Len Cranton and Petunia Road could never hold her. But that was something it seemed quite impossible to get into Len's stubborn head. So there he was now, chattering his way to Dunbarragh, making things just that much more difficult for her. Not that it could really matter greatly. Randy was done with her, hated the sight of her . . . a girl who had lead him on, wounded his pride and whose very existence imperiled the hopes he held most dear.

Tossing and turning, she watched the day brighten, and, when the stable clock struck six, she got up and dressed, unable to bear the burning acid of her thoughts any longer.

Going downstairs she found old Mrs. Costello in the hall, sweeping the vast expanse of stone floor rather fruitlessly with a flat shaped brush of bound straw. A "twig," this domestic implement was called, and indeed, Cathleen thought, if it had been no more than its name implied, it couldn't have been less use. Stirring the little furries of dust before her, the old woman looked up, her dark eyes bright in her wrinkled face.

"So you didn't go away with the Englishman?" she said softly, and without preamble.

"No," Cathleen answered, a little startled.

"It would be better for you if you did then," the old woman muttered. "There will be no luck for you staying in this place, for there is never any luck to them that will go against the dead! Miss Trenton," she whispered as though to herself, " 'twas the name put me off to begin with, but I was not long in doubt. You have the very look of her, the same bright, willful way with you. . . ."

"You mean, I am like her . . . my mother?"

"You are her very self over again. The years go backward for me when I look at you," the old woman sighed. "The old years and the old, old grief!" Kneeling now by the dusty hearth she seemed witchlike and forbidding, her gray locks falling around her face.

With a shiver of revulsion Cathleen slipped away through the open front door, leaving the old crone muttering to herself half-crazily. Perhaps Len had been right and it had been foolish of her to decide to remain here. Maybe she ought to have gone back with him and returned only when everything was settled in her favor—if that was how it was going to be. The next ten days were going to be a strain all around now that her identity had become public. She could see that with painful clarity. The animosity in old Mrs. Costello's mumbled remarks had been vaguely frightening. No luck for those who go against the wishes of the dead! Could that be true? Some buried streak of superstition in her Irish heart stirred and came to life at the question. She couldn't be quick enough then, hurrying through the quiet morning air, going she knew not where, only that it was a relief to walk, escaping from the great gray house behind her.

She took the shore road without thinking about it, only that it was vaguely soothing to look out over the glassy peaceful waters of the loch. Then presently she could hear footsteps behind her, and nervousness pricked once more. That thud-thudding of a man's heavy boots coming nearer and nearer; who could it be at this early hour in this utterly deserted spot, a farm laborer, perhaps, going to his day's work? Or some wild young blood returning from a night of poteen making on the islands? Forcing herself to look around at last, she saw the golden head of Lanty Conor. He raised a hand in greeting as she turned toward him calling out to her to wait. "I'm winded racing after you, Miss Cathleen, it is the rapid walker you are and no mistake," he announced as he drew level with her.

The sly familiarity of his manner offended her. His blue eyes gazed at her boldly as he smiled down at her, a giant of a young man with a stupidly handsome face, perfect as the features of some stone carved Grecian god—and just as insensitive.

"You wanted to catch up with me?" she questioned, with a haughty composure she was far from feeling.

"I'm after you ever since you went tearing out of the hall there. Was it what my old aunt said to you that upset you? Indeed then," he hurried on without waiting for her reply, "you don't want to mind her. There are plenty in this place that is on your side!"

"What do you mean?" Cathleen questioned uneasily.

"The Costellos," he said. "Your mother's own people by marriage. Only that mad old Mary Costello stands out against you for the grudge she bore your mother in the old times. But for the rest of us, it is a great day that brought you to Castle

Osborne! Now that the whole truth of your identity is out in the open, I can say that same to you." The blue eyes leered down at her. "It is proud I am to be walking at your side this minute, Cousin Cathleen!" he declared.

Cathleen stared at him, her thoughts in a turmoil, her pulse racing. "My cousin . . . you?" she stammered at last.

He nodded. "It was my own mother's brother that ran away with the Lady Sheila," he reminded her. "Why wouldn't we be cousins, then?"

She could think of no reply to that. Only that there was something wrong with it somewhere. She was no blood relation to this thrustful young man who now seemed to be urging her along with fresh purpose.

"Amn't I waiting for this chance ever since it was rumored who you were?" he told her triumphantly. "If we turn up there by the next cross roads it is the farm of the Costellos that will be before us. There they are, the whole clan of them, eager to meet you."

"It's very kind of them," Cathleen murmured, her uneasiness increasing, "but really . . . at this hour of the morning! Can't I call on them some other time?"

"Ah, sure, they're all up ages ago getting the men off to Dunbarragh fair," Lanty assured her. And seeing her still hesitate, he added softly, "The old people . . . my dead Uncle Mike's mother and father . . . you wouldn't refuse to see them, would you? You wouldn't disappoint them after all the sorrow the name of FitzOsborne brought to them in the days gone by?"

She saw the cottage then, set small and white within its boundary of neat low walls. The home of her mother's first husband . . . a husband so strangely chosen!

With a dreamlike feeling Cathleen approached the lonely isolated house, her feelings in chaos. This Lanty whom she instinctively distrusted—what was his motive for bringing her here?

CHAPTER TEN

THE OLD WOMAN who came forward to meet them wore a white frilled cap, tied under her chin, a paisley shawl crossed over her bosom and a crisp blue gingham apron. She had beautiful white wavy hair, blue eyes like Lanty's and features as perfectly formed. But there was nothing of Lanty's stupid insensitivity in the sweetness of her smile. Fragile and small she stood before them, the tremulous smile lighting her face, her work-worn hands held out. She didn't seem quite real . . . a figure out of a nursery picture book or a Hans Andersen fairy tale.

"Miss Sheila's child!" she said softly. "My poor Miss Sheila's own lamb! Come in, *asthore!* Come in, and welcome! Isn't this the great day for the Costellos!"

The gnarled hands held Cathleen's now, drawing her over the threshold into a wide pleasant room as spick-and-span as the old lady herself. The tiny windows, deep set in the thick white-washed wall, were curtained in crisp muslin, and on the sills stood pots of geraniums. The concrete floor had been scrubbed clean and the wide hearth swept free of ash. Peat burned under a great black kettle that swung from a hook in the cavernous chimney. There was a brown stoneware teapot on a little hob of loose stones beside the fire, and the long table set under the windows bore evidence of the meal eaten by the men of the family before their departure for the fair.

"I'm afraid it is a very early hour to call on you, Mrs. Costello," Cathleen offered, feeling her uneasiness begin to subside in the placid atmosphere of the little house.

"Indeed, then, there is no hour of the day or night, *asthore*, that you wouldn't be the same to me as the morning sun in the sky! Only that if I knew you were coming I'd have a fresh cake baked for you." Regretfully the old lady glanced at the enormous cartwheel of white soda bread on the table that had been cut into by the early breakfasters. "But the kettle is just on the boil," she comforted herself, "and I'll have a pot of tea wet for you in a minute."

Seizing an immense pair of bellows she began to blow the sods of peat piled under the swinging kettle, until a shower of golden sparks ran up out of them and the room was filled with the pungent smell of the earthy fuel.

"Sit down, *asthore*, sit down," she urged Cathleen as she went on with her puffing and blowing. "And run you out to the loft, Lanty, and see did the buff hen leave us an egg there."

Lanty gave Cathleen a companionable grin as he departed. "There's no hen in the world like the buff hen!" he explained. "Hasn't my grannie a houseful of eggs there in the crock on the dresser—but it's only the buff hen's egg that will do her when she has an honored visitor!"

" 'Tis a good egg the buff hen lays," the old lady agreed. Straightening from the hearth with the bellows in her hand, her blue eyes rested on Cathleen, mild and kind.

"But I don't want to take your eggs," Cathleen was saying. "I can have breakfast when I get back to the castle."

"Indeed, then, you'll eat your breakfast here at that table . . . where your mother ate it many a time before you," the old voice quavered, and Mrs. Costello lifted the corner of her apron to her eyes. "The same wild rose, you are, and the same grace about you . . . the same bright beauty that drew our poor Michaël— God rest him—from his home! Lanty was right when he told me that it was the ghost of Miss Sheila herself came back to us when you set foot in this place!"

Cathleen felt her own eyes mist over. "Tell me about my

mother, Mrs. Costello," she whispered. "I know so little about her, and . . . the other Mrs. Costello . . . the one at the castle, speaks of her so bitterly."

The white-frilled cap nodded. "That's Mary, my sister-in-law. Bewitched she was by her ladyship above at the castle, and where her ladyship hated, poor foolish Mary must hate, too. She was a hard woman, Lady FitzOsborne, putting her will over all those within her house, so that Mary had no life of her own, bearing her children here in this house and leaving them to me to rear. I had but two of my own, you see; Patch and Norah who married one of the Conors that's Lanty's father. But all Mary's children were like my own, and their own children after them. Matt Costello I reared and Michael his son. . . ."

Cathleen's brain began to reel with these ramifications of family history. "And Matt Costello, Michael's father, does he live here still?" she asked.

"He does, *asthore*. To Dunbarragh Fair he is gone this morning, but Kate, his wife, Michael's mother, is out in the top pasture milking the cow. She'll be here any minute. . . ."

"Did she, too, hate my mother?" Cathleen whispered.

"She did not," asserted old Mrs. Costello in her forthright way. "Why would she? It was only Mary above at the castle that had an unnatural heart for the poor lonely child, cast out by a proud mother that had no use for her, only pining for the son she never bore, flying in the face of God."

"And Sheila, my mother . . . she came here sometimes?"

"Like one of our own she was, and we loved her." Once more the old woman lifted the blue apron to her eyes. But the kettle boiling over at that moment demanded her attention, and Lanty came in with the golden-brown egg that had been obligingly laid by the buff hen.

Seated on the settle by the hearth Cathleen sat silent while the tea was made, the egg put into a small smoky pan to boil. Somehow the picture was shaping, the pattern falling into place.

The marriage that had puzzled her so deeply . . . . suddenly she was beginning to understand how simply, how almost inevita-- bly it had come about. This kindly little farmhouse that had been her mother's childhood refuge . . . the numerous boy and girl Costellos with whom she had played. She would have known Michael Costello for years before he emerged as the dashing young horseman who had come from Lord Dunlargan's stables to teach her to ride. . . .

A shadow fell across the open doorway then and a woman appeared, carrying two brimming cans of milk, hung from a yoke across her shoulders. Kate Costello . . . Sheila FitzOs- borne's onetime mother-in-law—a tall, hardily built woman with graying hair and an almost disconcertingly direct glance for the stranger.

"So you brought her, Lanty!" Kate said, needing apparently no word of introduction to explain the girl on the settle. Lowering the pails of milk carefully to the floor, she disen- tangled herself from the yoke and, unsmilingly, held out her hand. With a nervous tremor Cathleen took it. There was something intimidating about the haughty dignity of this peasant woman, who with quiet composure surveyed her. "You are very like your poor mother," she said, "there is no look of Michael about you at all."

"But how could there be?" Cathleen's heart gave a frightened lurch. "Michael was not my father. My mother married again after his death, you know. . . ."

"Ah, yes, I believe she did. We heard something of the kind," Kate returned, but there was no conviction in her tone.

They think I'm Michael's daughter . . . and they're going to go on thinking it," Cathleen decided in horror. "My name," she said hurriedly, "is Trenton."

Kate nodded. "So Lanty was telling us," she agreed, with the air of one humoring an obstinate child.

Scooping the warm milk from one of the pails, old Mrs.

Costello began pouring out tea. "Come up to the table now, Miss Cathleen," she invited. "Will I pour you a cup of tea, too, Lanty?"

"You needn't bother," Lanty answered with a grin. "I'll have a drop out of the bottle." Going to the great dresser that almost filled the inner wall of the room, he groped in a drawer and drew out a flask filled with thick white liquid and with a wink and a nod at Cathleen poured himself a cupful of the stuff. "Poteen," he exclaimed brazenly. "Like to taste it?"

"No, thank you." In spite of herself Cathleen's voice was rigid with disapproval, and she saw Kate shrug in disgust.

"At this hour of the morning, Lanty! You ought to be ashamed of yourself!" She turned to Cathleen. " 'Tis the curse of the men in this country, that same poteen," she mourned.

"Ah, now don't be hard on him, Kate," the old woman put in. "It is a grand drink for putting the life into a person in the hard hours of the morning."

"A drink that will take life as quickly as give it," Kate said quietly. "It was the death of Michael and many a one before him . . . it will be the death of Lanty if he doesn't put a curb on himself."

That she had spoken thus deliberately of her son's death there could be no doubt. The honest eyes met Cathleen's timid glance squarely. "Your poor mother, God rest her, didn't have much luck in her first marriage," she said softly. "Though Mike was my own son, there was nothing but pity in my heart for Sheila FitzOsborne the night she stepped into a boat there on the shores of the lough and sailed away with him. Wild, he was, as the west wind, and as wayward. . . ."

"That is not how Mary Costello at the castle speaks of him. She blames my mother for his death," Cathleen said, in a small shaken voice.

Kate nodded. "Lanty has told us the way she does be railing at you. It is hard for you in a house full of strangers, and you no more than a child. But in this house you will find a welcome always awaiting you '' A hard brown hand came down on Cathleen's shoulder. ''Don't forget that, now. Come over any time you are lonesome . . . the way your mother came here before you.''

There were little murmurs of assent to this, from old Mrs. Costello and Cathleen felt her heart swell with quick gratitude. How kind and disarming they were, these simple folk, and how wrong she had been to suspect Lanty's motives in bringing her here!

And yet as she walked home with him half an hour later she found herself disliking him as much as ever. After the pleasant interlude in the farm kitchen, that simple but delicious breakfast, the poetic ramblings of the old grandmother and the quiet, sensible conversation of the dignified Kate, Lanty's bold familiarity seemed increasingly repugnant. It was one thing to be claimed in kinship by the gentle, perfectly mannered Costello women, quite another to have this brash boy with the smell of drink on his breath leering at her with his hard blue eyes, addressing her with scarcely veiled insolence.

Was she just being a frightful snob, Cathleen wondered, trying to control her revulsion when presently Lanty's hand came out to help her over a stile in the way. They were returning to the castle by a shortcut that led through the Osborne lands. Resting a moment on the top of the stile, Cathleen looked out over the great expanse of mountain and moorland. Sun turned the lough waters to sparkling silver, touching the wooded islands to emerald life.

For a moment Lanty stood silent, as though sharing her quiet wonder at the beauty of the scene. Then he said, in a low voice, ''All these acres coming to you, Cathleen! What are you going to do with them?''

Startled, she felt the blood rise in her cheeks. Not once in the Costello household had the matter of her inheritance been mentioned—indeed in that atmosphere of simple friendliness she had almost forgotten the more troublesome implications of her FitzOsborne background. Childishly, perhaps, she had been grateful to accept the affection of the Costello family at its face value. They had loved her mother . . . and for her mother's sake welcomed her. But now something sly and calculating in Lanty's stupidly handsome face made her hesitate before asking unhappily, "What do you mean?"

"The Costellos there in their little bit of a house," he said. "And you with your great castle. The Costellos with no more than a score of half-acre stony fields between the lot of them, and you with the whole width of the countryside in your keep! Isn't it time for you to be remembering all that was done for your mother by those that sometimes were hard put to it to find food for their own? But no matter how hard the seasons might be and no matter how short the drop of milk or the flour and the butter Sheila FitzOsborne would find the best set before her on that very table where you ate your fill just now."

"But of course I realize how good they were to my mother . . . and of course I am grateful . . . " Cathleen began in bewilderment.

" 'Tis not only a question of gratitude, but of family obligation," Lanty said, a sullen look coming over his face. "Blood is thicker than water. You are nearer to the Costellos than you are to those pushing, grasping Kilmorans. Don't forget that, and you shouting around the place for all to hear that you want to give the half of the estate to that fellow Randy! It isn't gratitude we want . . . but land. . . . "

For a moment Cathleen was too horrified to speak, then controlling the surge of anger that made her pulse pound, she said quietly, "How dare you speak of your employer, Mr. Kilmoran, in this way . . . and to me! I may be indebted to the Costello family for their kindness to my mother in her child-hood, and that is something I shall never forget . . . whether I inherit my grandmother's estate or not. But you . . . ! To you I owe nothing. Nor do I like your insolent manner. . . ."

With a snort of sardonic laughter Lanty interrupted her. "So you owe me nothing! That's a good one! We'll see what you owe me before we're through!"

"In the meantime," Cathleen said hotly, inwardly dismissing this pitiful attempt at bluff with the scorn it deserved, "I would suggest that you get back to the castle and see to Miss Mollie's breakfast. I'm not coming in yet." Lightly she swung herself down from the stile and turned aside from the path to climb the rough hillside.

"Too proud to be seen by the castle folk walking with me, eh?" called Lanty after her. "All right, go on my proud young lady. Climb your grand hill with your head in the air. I'll have you groveling at my feet before I'm done with you." He was shaking his fist at her retreating form now, his face purple, his voice thick. "And there's one more thing I'm telling you, I'll die rather than let that fellow Randy have one inch or one ell of the Osborne land! Only waiting to throw me out, is he? Only waiting to sack me? 'Tis himself that will be thrown out in penniless dishonor. . . ."

He was drunk, Cathleen decided with a tremor of nervous disgust, remembering the cupful of raw spirits he had poured into his breakfastless stomach. If he had not been drunk he would never have talked in this crazy threatening way. When he had sobered up again he would most likely have no recollection of the dreadful things he had said. Comforting herself with this reflection, she wandered along a little sheep track through the cushions of bell heather and patches of bright green moss. Even on the high hills these areas of soggy bogland abounded, the water forever draining away in tiny tinkling streams that filled the air with their music. And nowhere was it altogether safe to cross even the most innocent looking stretch of ground unless there was a beaten path before you. Randy had told Cathleen this on the evening they climbed the Doon Hill to the cowman's cabin, the bright green patches with their blowing tufts of fairy bog cotton that looked so attractive could so easily hide a morass that meant the horror of a slow sinking to suffocation.

Remembering his words now with a shiver, she couldn't help thinking how much the Irish resembled their own wild hills. This smiling landscape with its hidden snares! But surely, surely, the welcome of the charming Costello women this morning had held no lurking treachery! No, she couldn't . . . she wouldn't let herself think such things! Honesty had shone so clearly from Kate Costello's eyes and old Mrs. Costello had seemed so full of love. It was only Lanty who was false hearted and horrible. And there was nothing new in that discovery. She had distrusted him all along.

With a sigh she turned around, making for the castle, thinking with distaste of the inevitable encounters with Lanty that lay ahead. Supposing things did work out in her favor during the next ten days and she was forced to accept the ownership of the estate, Lanty Conor was going to be a problem indeed. Just how he might be disposed of she couldn't quite see, for dismissing him from the castle service would solve nothing. He would simply lurk in the district then, a dangerous enemy. Oh, dear, how full of problems the life of an heiress could be! Especially an heiress with so mixed a family history. Here she was bound by incalculable ties not only to her kinsfolk the Kilmorans, but also to the humble kindly Costellos, whom—apart from Lanty—she would be only too glad to help. But was one allowed to carve an estate up in slices and hand in around to all and sundry? Weren't there all sorts of restrictions when you administered an ancient property—deeds, entails, goodness only knew what. Randy had spoken ponderously of court injunctions. Oh, well, she could ask Mr. Philligan to advise her if she found herself in the awkward position of potential benefactor to half the county!

Entering the big gloomy hall with its stone paving and dusty antlers, she found Mollie kneeling on the floor in earnest conversation with an assortment of dogs, who, squatting on their haunches like lions grouped around a lion tamer, regarded her earnestly. The child's face was pale with concentration, her green eyes wide. On her shoulder, the Siamese kitten crouched looking equally absorbed.

"I'm just introducing Yo-Yo to the dogs," Mollie explained, "they've had to live in the stableyard ever since he came, and it isn't fair. Randy has been awfully patient about it. But it can't go on forever. . . ." Lowering the kitten to the ground, she said, "Look Yo-Yo, nice dogs, good dogs!" She patted them in turn, the mastiff, the setter and the solemn bassett hound.

Yo-Yo confronted by these monsters fluffed out his tail and spat. The dogs uttered low whinning sounds, their long faces wearing expressions of comical embarrassment and discomfort. A brown paw shot out, catching the bassett smartly on the nose. The dog blinked patiently and whined a little louder, but made no retaliation. Mollie picked Yo-Yo up in her arms with an optimistic, "Well, that's a beginning, anyway. They know now Yo-Yo isn't a kitchen cat to be chased, and Yo-Yo will soon learn he mustn't spit at them and try to box their ears, Siamese are supposed to get on awfully well with dogs when they become accustomed to them."

"Good dogs!" she praised, with pats of dismissal, a special fondling for the long-suffering bassett hound. "Now out! All of you!" She pointed to the open door and the dogs padded off obediently. Yo-Yo, encouraged by the sight of their retreating forms, struggled from Mollie's arms to follow them. "See, he likes them already. He's just longing to get acquainted!" the child exulted. "He'll be off hunting with them before we know where we are . . . only that we'll probably be gone from Castle Osborne by the time the grouse shooting begins." A shadow crossed the small vivid face. "Cathleen, what are you going to do with the gun dogs when we leave?" she asked.

"When you leave? What on earth are you talking about? You aren't leaving."

"How is it all going to work out then?"

"I don't know. But it *will* work out. Let's go and have breakfast." Cathleen said, a little sharply. She'd had enough problems hurled at her head for one morning and wasn't going to start on a long fruitless discussion with Mollie on the pros and cons of the missing will. Neither was she going to mention to the chatterbox child that she had already breakfasted with the Costellos, her mind boggling at the prospect of the endless explanations the announcement would undoubtedly involve.

But the day that had begun so disturbingly was to become one of the most memorable of that dramatic summer. Soon afer breakfast the girls set out to tramp over the hills, a lunch of sandwiches in the pockets of the capacious raincoats it was never safe to venture far without. Crossing the Doon Hill they came to the higher range beyond, and by noon the great stretch of three counties lay at their feet. Sitting on a high bog with a drying peat stack for shelter, they ate their sandwiches in the dreamy content of shared physical fatigue. It was a day of broken white cloud and softly brilliant light, the cloud shadows running away over the sloping valleys and shining lough. They could take the Sky Road when they had rested, Mollie suggested, follow it over the mountains until it dropped down into Osbornestown. "We could have dinner at the Angler's then, and Randy would take us home in the car. He's bound to be there before dark. All market days end up at the Angler's for Randy and his pals."

Listening to the bees in the heather at her feet, Cathleen agreed drowsily to this plan. Anything that kept them away from the castle and an evening meal served by Lanty Conor was welcome . . . even if it meant enduring the sullen glances of Randy, who might not be altogether pleased to find them at the Angler's Hotel.

"Poor Randy!" Mollie was saying, rolling over in the soft peaty loam. "How he loathed your boyfriend last night!"

"Len Cranton . . . he's not my boyfriend, exactly," Cathleen interposed mildly.

"I'm glat to hear it!" Mollie offered pertly. "And I bet Randy would be, too. He didn't think much of Mr. Cranton's arrival . . . but, of course, he was mad jealous. Romantic, isn't it! All these men being crazy over you . . . anyone could see the way that poor Len felt! I wish I were twenty-one . . . fifteen is such a boring age . . . people, specially men, refusing to believe you are grown-up."

"Mollie dear! For a grown-up, I must say, you talk some pretty thick nonsense!" Cathleen laughed. She couldn't keep the sudden happiness out of her tone. Had Randy been jealous of Len? Did he still care enough to be jealous? Tramping along high above the world with the golden hours of the afternoon wheeling over her, her spirits rose and soared. This shining air, like wine on her lips, and the singing streams beside her . . . cares dwindled, nerves and brain went slack lulled by the rhythm of that day-long march.

In a mindless glow of delicious fatigue she sat at twilight in the Angler's bar drinking an iced lime juice that tasted like ambrosia. Here were the fishing holiday people again in their waders and Windbreakers, and Mrs. Callaghan bustling in to welcome Mollie, her glance darting uneasily to Cathleen, as her work-worn hand came out in greeting. "Indeed, then, Miss Trenton, I'm delighted to see you. Is it Miss Trenton I should say . . . or Miss FitzOsborne? Isn't it the wonder of the world the way things turned out for you? The whole town is full of it. . . ."

"I bet it is, too!" Mollie sighed when, after a few more congratulatory and rather two-edged remarks, Mrs. Callaghan had left them. "I'd forgotten the quick way gossip gets around this place—and such meaty gossip, too!"

That was the end of all mindless content. Nervously now

Cathleen was aware of the curious glances coming their way, the whispered comments. When they'd waited in the bar almost an hour with no sign of Randy, Mollie went out into the twilight street to look for him. He had made his homeward halt perhaps at the humbler establishment higher up the village street—the small shebeen in which the cattle drovers drank their thick glasses of porter.

Returning to Cathleen, the child's face was wan with weariness and hunger. "We'll have to have dinner without him," she announced. "He has gone home. I met Festy Dolan, the mailman, who has just seen him drive straight through Osbornestown and off down the Castle Road. But, of course, he wouldn't come here tonight . . . having more sense than we have he'd have realized the way the talk about us is going around, and he'd *hate* it."

Cathleen went a little pale. "How are we going to get home then?" It was a good seven miles to the castle gates, another mile up the long drive, and already they had both walked to the limit of their endurance.

"Lanty Conor will take us," Mollie announced. "I've fixed it up with him. He's out there in the yard with the pipers. . . ."

"The pipers?" Cathleen asked, limp with dismay.

"There's going to be a bit of a Ceilidh here tonight for the guests . . . that is a kind of Gaelic concert and dance. Mrs. Callaghan often arranges it on a Friday night; gets the local boys in to sing the old songs and teach the visitors the round dances, the reels and jigs and things. And Lanty is one of her best performers, a marvelous step dancer. You'll like it, it's fun, though I'm afraid it will be a bit late by the time Lanty is ready to drive us home in the dreadful old borrowed Ford wagon he has got out there."

CHAPTER ELEVEN

IN SPITE OF HER HUNGER Cathleen didn't enjoy the excellent dinner very much—grilled trout all pink and tender, a trout that had been swimming the lough waters only that morning, slices of mountain lamb swimming in its own rich gravy and flanked by new green peas, and sauté potatoes. There was a cream dessert to follow, and it was Mrs. Callaghan herself who came in with the bottle of chilled sweet Sauterne. "With the compliments of the house," she murmured, "to the new owner of Castle Osborne!" Pouring out three glasses she lifted one to her own lips. "Your very good health, Miss Trenton . . . or is it Miss Costello, I should be saying?"

"Thank you, Mrs. Callaghan," Cathleen murmured in hot confusion, aware of the interested glances from neighboring tables. "It is Miss Trenton, though, not Costello."

"She thinks you're Michael Costello's daughter!" Mollie whispered, wide-eyed, when Mrs. Callaghan had withdrawn. "I wonder where she got *that* quaint idea?"

Keeping her lips grimly shut, Cathleen looked down the long dining room where, at a table near the kitchen serving door, Lanty and his fellow dancers were eating. There were bottles of whiskey before them, and already Lanty's rough voice could be heard rising wild and uncontrolled above the general buzz of conversation that filled the crowded room. Heaven alone knew what state he would be in before the evening was over!

With a suppressed shiver of fear she turned to Mollie.

"Couldn't we go home by taxi or something?" she begged. "Lanty is going to be hopelessly drunk by the look of him."

"Oh, the dancing will sober him up,' Mollie returned calmly. "And I don't suppose we'd get a hired car this side of Dunbarragh. They all go to the big cattle market, and most of them make a night of it, staying around Dunbarragh picking up fares as long as the gas holds out. So unless we walk it, we'll have to wait for Lanty. Quite frankly, I don't think I could walk . . . I've an enormous blister on one heel. . . ."

"Won't Randy be worried about you and . . . wonder where you are?" Cathleen tried then.

Mollie shook her red gold head. "Mrs. Costello will tell him we were going to tramp over the hills to the Sky Road, and he'll guess we came down by Osbornestown. Maybe he'll come back presently to look for us."

But Randy didn't come to look for them. And after a while Cathleen gave up watching the swing doors in flurries of nervous expectancy, and settled down to the spectacle before her.

The small dining tables had been set back against the walls now and the floor cleared. On a chair near the serving door sat an old man nursing a large melodeon, and presently, with a flourish the serving door opened and the pipers marched in, two tall young men in saffron kilts with massive silver Tara pins catching the dark green scarves at their shoulders.

There was an outburst of clapping, a wild war whoop or two from the audience as the strange heart-curdling lament of the pipes began. Most of the waders and Windbreakers had been discarded now, and the women guests shone forth in the colored splendor of evening dresses, their suntanned faces glowing with health and laughter, their carefully arranged coiffeurs gleaming as hair only can gleam in the moist sweetness of Connemara air.

Suddenly conscious of their shabby sweaters and old skirts,

the travel stains of the long day still upon them, Cathleen whispered to Mollie that she felt most frightfully dowdy. And Mrs. Callaghan had insisted upon placing them at a prominent table, right on the edge of the dance floor.

"The lady of Castle Osborne!" teased Mollie. "You can afford to be shabby."

"Don't!" winced Cathleen, eyeing the festive Sauterne with distaste.

"Randy would kill us," offered Mollie somberly, "if he knew we were here making a show of ourselves before all the gossips of Osbornestown . . . and Mrs. Callaghan asking you at the top of her voice if you are a Miss Costello! We'd better not tell him *that* bit!"

"We'll tell him *nothing*. If we ever get home alive!" groaned Cathleen, as "The Wearing of the Green" came to an end with a long mournful mooing sound.

"Areesh! Areesh!" cried the enraptured audience with a stamping of feet and clapping of hands. But the pipers, refusing the encore, disappeared through the serving door, and the old man drew his melodeon out full length and plunged into a rollicking jig. Now the dancers appeared, four awkward-seeming young men in their working clothes and heavy boots, Lanty's bright yellow head and flushed handsome face standing out strikingly. For a moment or two, like timid swimmers on a river's brink, the young men hesitated, while the music grew louder and wilder. Then all at once, as though moved by a single will, the four pairs of heavy boots began a soft tapping and the intricacies of the jig unfolded.

Arms held straight down by their sides, their bodies rigid, their faces fixed and blank, the four men beat out the intricate rhythm with feet so light that they scarcely seemed to touch the floor. A miracle that they scarcely seemed to touch the floor, a miracle of controlled and classic grace, passionless as the dancing of ancient Greece and yet holding in its excitingly repeated emphasis something of the hypnotism of an African ritual.

Cathleen drew in a long satisfied breath as the jig ended, to be followed by an eight-handed reel, danced to an intoxicating tune that set her own feet tapping under the table. How superbly Lanty moved through the elaborate figures! She could almost forget how much she disliked him! But the floor was clear again now, the melodeon plunging into the "Rakes of Mallow."

"Ladies and gentlemen!" called a booming voice from somewhere. "Take your partners from the Lancers." Cathleen looked up to see Lanty standing by her side. "Will you dance this with me, miss?" he asked diffidently enough, though there was a gleam of tipsy malice in his blue eyes. Cathleen just stared at him in frozen horror. Somehow she had never imagined anything so awful as this emerging from the mixed experiences of the evening.

"Go on, Cathleen, don't be a spoilsport," Mollie whispered. "Everyone dances with everyone on these occasions, and Lanty is the best dancer in the room."

With a sense of bewilderment Cathleen was on her feet. She could *feel* the interested eyes watching her on all sides. The heiress of Castle Osborne getting up to dance with the servant who, if rumor was right, was in all probability her cousin. But to have refused Lanty in his half-tipsy state might have started a scene it would have been much more difficult to endure. Besides, the Lancers, she consoled herself, was an impersonal kind of dance, in which you changed partners so often that the one you started with hardly counted.

They were off then—and in spite of herself Cathleen soon began to enjoy the lively exercise, Lanty guiding her expertly through the mazes of the dance. Light as thistledown on his feet, his yellow hair flaming around his handsome head, his blue eyes blazing, she could not but be aware of the intentness, the mischief of his glances as he whispered his instructions. When he swung her in the closing crescendo of the first figure, his arms were tight around her and his lips came close to her ear. "Listen to me, Miss Cathleen!" he said urgently. "I've got to talk to you sometime soon. Make a chance tonight for me to have a word with you, alone. It's time you and I understood one another."

Breathless with the dance, lifted off her feet by the strong arms that swung her around in midair, she did not answer him. It was all too mad. There was no answer she could make, and before she had time to collect her senses, she found herself being thrust across the floor with an urgent push from Lanty and the injunction to, "Go on, now, miss, and off with you into the ladies' chain!"

When once more he claimed her, he began at once his eagerly muttered pleadings, his whiskey-laden breath hot in her face. "Maybe you thought it was poteen talking this morning, Cathleen, but I wasn't drunk then any more than I'm drunk now," he insisted.

With a shiver of distaste she drew away from him. "You are *drunk*," she whispered, "that's the only thing that makes any excuse for the crazy rubbish you talked this morning—the way you are going on now!"

She saw the dull flush of anger stain his fair skin.

"Listen to me!" he hissed threatingly. "If I have a sup of whiskey taken it's neither here nor there. I'm a Connaught man with a hard head, and a hard heart, too, when it comes to fighting for me rights. And I'm going to fight for them! Let me tell you, me proud Cathleen, I could break you in two if so I wished, for I hold your fate in the hollow of me hand . . . so put that in your pipe and smoke it!"

Once more she escaped from him, her pulses pounding nervously as she floundered through this maddest set of Lancers she had ever known. If only she had the courage to break away, rush out on the tide of wild music and flee through the doorway into the quiet night. . . . But the thought of Lanty's rough strong hands waiting for her at the end of the "chain," the sight of his mad blue eyes fixed on her, gave to the moment a touch of nightmare that confused her senses, robbing her of all power of decision. So that once more she found herself in his arms, heard him murmur as the dance ended that he would be waiting for her on the river bridge at the end of the village street. "Come out to me as soon as you can, my dear, or it will be the worse for you! It is a square thing to me if you haven't the courage even to listen to the just case I have to put before you."

Going back to her table, his last words ringing in her ears with their challenge to the qualities she most valued, she found Mollie had disappeared, and saw that she had joined a group of friends by the bar. Courage . . . a sense of justice . . . what instinct had prompted Lanty to taunt her with the lack of these? Absently sipping the wine grown flat and warm in its glass, she told herself she had no intention of keeping the crazy tryst he had suggested. All the melodramatic nonsense about breaking her . . . holding her fate in the hollow of his hands! Was he really as mad as he sounded, or was there some substance, some purpose behind his treatenings? "It isn't gratitude we want, but land!" he had stormed at her this morning. But they were all land-crazy, the landless Irish. A dispossessed people crying through the centuries for the soil defiled by foreign occupation. All the music and the singing tonight had held the same plaintive note of yearning—folk songs born of tears and poverty.

Passing her hand across her brow, Cathleen tried to steady her thoughts and steel her heart with reason. Lanty in the darkness out there waiting for her where the trout stream whispered beneath the arched stone bridge. Well let him wait! What he had to say to her, just or unjust, could be equally well spoken in daylight, at some more seemly time. Lighting a cigarette, her fingers trembled. Like a magnet drawing her she could feel those blue eyes piercing the night, watching the door of the hotel. And presently, as though she moved in her sleep, she was on ther feet, slipping out of the noisy room and down the long narrow corridor, her heart lightening unaccountably as though eased of some burden by the decisive action. There was laughter in her eyes as she unlatched the door. Probably all Lanty wanted to tell her was that he would set the banshees on her if she didn't present him with the half of the Osborne lands forthwith.

Running across the village street she felt utterly foolish. The houses opposite the hotel were small and thatched, the stars high above the humble crouching roofs. In the dim light she could just make out the lane that led behind the cottages to the river's edge, one of the numerous small trout streams that flowed from the marshy mountain lands to feed the great lake—a lonely and deserted spot. With a shiver of apprehension Cathleen saw the shadowy bulk of the young man awaiting her. "You did well to come," was his dryly spoken greeting, and as he cupped his hands around the flame of the match that lit his cigarette she saw his face, grim and strong boned, in the momentary illumination.

"Smoke?"

She could feel rather than see the crushed package of cigarettes he held out to her. Her refusal was curt. "What is it you want to say to me?" she demanded, in a tone calculated to quell any sociable preamble—like shared cigarettes.

Lanty laughed shortly. "You can get off your high horse, me dear, and tell me just how much Castle Osborne means to you? Only a few days now, I understand, and they'll be handing it over to you lock, stock and barrel. But there's many a thing can go wrong in the space of a few days."

"Such as?" Cathleen interposed quietly.

"The inconvenient bit of paper that would name the upstart heir. Mind you, I'd die rather than see that happen, as I told you this morning. Randy Kilmoran isn't getting the Osborne lands if I can help it . . . but neither are you unless you take care."

But Cathleen was hardly listening to the last part of this strange announcement, her heart turning over with a sickening thud. The missing will . . . Lanty knew something about it! Why hadn't she thought of that possibility before? Excitement raced in her blood—a queer exhilaration that had nothing to do with the material aspects of the situation and was somehow wholly concerned with Randy. If the will were to turn up after all . . . if she herself were the person to unearth it! The very thought loosened the tight bands of misery that had constricted her heart ever since that awful afternoon in the library when she had in almost so many words accused Randy of being a calculating gold digger—that afternoon when she had seen the light go out of his eyes and watched him turn from her in loathing! Oh, if only she were going to be given a chance to undo the mischief she had wrought that fateful day! To be able to go to Randy and say, "Look, Randy . . . I don't come into this at all; Castle Osborne is yours, and I've found the proof of that fact. I've never wanted the estate. I've only wanted you to have what my grandmother intended for you. Everything else you've thought about me has been a ghastly mistake." Surely he would realize then that her misunderstanding of his lovemaking had arisen from sheer muddle and bewilderment. . . . At least he would know that she wanted the best for him; put his welfare before her own. And if that in itself wasn't enough to give him an inkling as to the real nature of her feeling for him, she would have the satisfaction of going away with the knowledge that she had been instrumental in reinstating him in the place that he loved—a bleak enough prospect, perhaps, but *something*.

She came back to earth with a sigh, aware that Lanty was eyeing her earnestly above the glowing tip of his cigarette. "A fellow," he was saying, "who might tell you something that would be greatly to your advantage, if so be you were ready to do a little deal with him."

"What fellow?" Cathleen demanded, with the bewilderment of the wool-gathering listener. "I thought we were talking about Lady FitzOsborne's lost will."

Lanty put a none too gentle hand on her arm. "For the love of Mike, miss, don't go shouting it out like that—you wouldn't know who might chance to be listening to us!" he whispered in a horrified undertone. "All I was saying to you was that I could put you in touch with a fellow who might be able to help you to consolidate your position—if you know what I mean."

"I don't. It's all about as clear as mud. Who is this mysterious friend of yours?"

"A chap that lives over on one of the lake islands."

"And he knows something about the will?"

"It's not for me to be telling you what he knows. He'll tell you that himself in return for the thing it is he wants of you."

"Oh!" Cathleen breathed softly. "So there's a bargain in it?"

"There is to be sure. You can hear the details for yourself if you meet me tomorrow morning down by the lough quay. I'll row you over to the island. Keep your mouth shut about all this if you value your own interests. And we'd better make our journey early—before the Kilmorans are astir. Can you meet me at half six?"

Cathleen's heart gave an uneasy lurch. To go off with this impudent Lanty in the dawn to a desolate island where some unknown villain lurked . . . for, of course, there was villainy afoot; the whole thing reeked of intrigue. Information about the missing will in exchange for some concession she was supposed to make. Just what was she letting herself in for? But even while she hesitated, she knew there was no possibility of refusing Lanty's sinister invitation. He—and his unsavory friend—knew something about the missing will, that was clear enough. For Randy's sake it was up to her to find out as much as she could. *For Randy's sake!* Her voice was soft as a sigh of love, saying, "I'll be down at the quay at six-thirty, Lanty."

"And not a word to anyone, mind!" he warned again, as she turned away.

Running back to the hotel she felt elated and a little afraid. But elation was uppermost, so that as she entered the hotel once more her cheeks glowed and her blue eyes shone. Whatever else came of it, by this time tomorrow she would have the key to Lanty's odd behavior, his hints and threats and innuendoes. By this time tomorrow perhaps the missing will would be in her hands! A crazy hope, no doubt, but the whole situation was crazy—Lanty and his unknown confederate and the bargain they wanted to drive with her, a bargain, of course, concerning the disposal of the Osborne property. *But they've no hold on me*, she thought in easy triumph, *I can hear what it is they have to say and go my own way.* And that would be straight back to Randy with whatever information she had contrived to collect. If only it could be information, clear, conclusive and altogether to his benefit!

In a glow of love and self-sacrifice she stood hesitant on the threshold of the noisy dining room ballroom. Somewhere a radio amplifier was blaring out music from a Dublin dance band. Everyone was dancing this modern dance, the Gaelic contingent, including the kilted pipers, having retired to the bar in the adjoining room, and looking through the door in an effort to locate Mollie, Cathleen found herself being hailed by a very mellow Mr. Callaghan.

"Ah, there you are, Miss Trenton. The very lady we were looking for! Amn't I after opening a bottle of my best champagne for you this very minute!"

Taking her arm, the old gentleman led her to an animated group of which Mollie was the center. In the spate of introductions that followed, Cathleen found her heart sinking. County neighbors had heard her romantic story and wanted to meet her, and Mollie was child enough to enjoy the moment with its little stir of notoriety—the Lagans from Clanlagen House, the other side of the lough; Tony O'Hara, who managed the village bank; Tommy Rafferty, who "mastered" the local hunt; the three lively Driscoll girls who lived in what had once been a pirate's castle on a peninsula in the roaring Atlantic twenty miles away. Real kindliness as well as a shrewd curiosity shone on the friendly faces as greetings were spoken. "Well, I hope there'll be high doings when we have a young mistress once more at Osborne!" a Driscoll girl giggled.

"To the lovely chatelaine of Castle Osborne!" cried old Mr. Callaghan dramatically at this point, raising his glass of champagne.

"May I drink that toast, too?" came a quiet voice at the bar door as Randy Kilmoran strode in. For a moment there was an electrified and awkward silence while Cathleen felt the blood fly to her cheeks. Oh, if only the floor would open and quietly swallow her up! Randy's fixed smile, the flicker of malice in his eyes as he met her confused and appealing glance. He would think . . . that she had come here to the Angler's to gloat in public over his downfall and her own triumph. How could he help thinking it? All the fine feelings with which she came from her interview with Lanty shriveled and died, leaving her shamed and lost.

"Only that it's rather a premature toast, isn't it?" she managed to blurt, her trembling words quite drowned by old Mr. Callaghan's heartily welcome to the new arrival.

"Kilmoran himself! The welcome of the house to ye, sir, and if it's a backhanded compliment to yourself to be drinking a toast to the new owner of your own home, aren't you a big enough man to take it in your stride?"

"I hope so, Tim," Randy returned gravely, taking the glass of champagne the old man handed to him, and raising it with a ceremonial gesture. "To Cathleen . . . and Castle Osborne!" he said softly. There were sudden tears in Cathleen's eyes, and for a moment she fought back the impulse to turn and rush out of the hotel. Only that Randy was beside her now, smiling down at her. She could hardly believe she was hearing right when he whispered, ''That's a good tune they're relaying—come on and dance!''

He lifted his shoulders in an imperceptible shrug. ''Couldn't have you bursting into tears at Callagan's bar on top of all the other sensations that are abroad about the family. How did you get let in for this gabfeast?''

''All this ghastly 'toasting,' and so on? I don't know. The Callaghans seemed to get the bit between their teeth the moment Mollie and I appeared this evening. First it was a bottle of Sauterne at dinner—then the champagne. Old Callaghan sprang it on us quite without warning. I was out of the room when Mollie collected what seems to be the entire county, all agog with the story of the newly discovered heiress. I just hadn't the savoir faire, I suppose, to know how to deal with the situation. It's all so silly!''

Falteringly, Cathleen told him how it had come about that Mollie and she had not had the same good sense. ''Mollie was so sure you'd be here, and we were pretty whacked after our tramp over the mountains. I wouldn't have come within miles of the place if I'd realized what I was letting myself in for.''

''Something you'd have to go through ultimately, anyhow,'' Randy offered, with a tone of unconcern that she felt didn't ring quite true. And it was solely to comfort him that she blurted out, ''Aren't you taking too much for granted—just like the Callaghans? I'm not yet the heiress of Castle Osborne....'' And passionately she added, ''I never want to be!''

''We won't start on that angle of it, if you don't mind,'' Randy returned stiffly. And then somehow all at once she was aware of his arm tightening around her as the dreamy tide of music bore them along. Nothing mattered suddenly but his nearness and the magic harmony of their movements. How easily, of its own accord, her body seemed to respond to his guidance. This moment, this music that made them one, so that she knew without conscious thought, that for him, too, the hypnotic sweetness was all. Half closing her eyes she let herself drift without effort in his arms.

It was cruel in the end that he should spoil it. Quite clearly she could feel his change of mood, still holding her close, but yet in some undefinable way abandoning her as he said, "You haven't asked how your boyfriend fared this morning. He caught the Dublin train quite comfortably. I went to the station with him; he sent you his salaams . . . his love."

"Thank you." Her voice was tired and small. "It was good of you to . . . take him to the station." *And how could I have forgotten all about Len so quickly,* she was asking herself in the bleak silence that followed. Len with his voluble all too confiding nature, chattering his way to Dunbarragh in the chill dawn. Len fighting for his own hand—and fighting cunningly. He had underlined the significance of his visit by that last message—despatched by Randy. He had sent his love. And last night in the twilight he had held her in his arms while Randy passed them by. How silly to have forgotten in the magic of the dance how heavily the dice were loaded against her. Not only Castle Osborne, but Len was her enemy.

He had really come only to take them home, Randy reminded her as the dance ended, and she noticed how he avoided a return to that too convivial bar, calling to Mollie from the door, reminding them both a trifle wearily as they piled into the waiting car, that he had had a long day and a heavy one. He talked of the fair as they drove over the rough lake road. He had bought eight young Hereford bullocks. But there was little jubilation in his tone and Cathleen for all the effort she made couldn't summon up any real enthusiasm. Not all the Herefords in the world could comfort her tonight, nor, it seemed, could they greatly interest Randy, yawning sleepily at her side.

Only in the thought of Lanty Conor did a gleam of bleak

comfort come, as presently she climbed into the vast four-poster bed. When the heart is young there is always tomorrow! She did not ask herself if she had been wise in the making of so bizarre a rendezvous. Would the journey at dawn over the lonely waters of the lough bring danger to her? She hardly cared. It was for Randy's sake she was undertaking it; that gave it glory beyond all timorous foreboding. Drifting off to sleep she was hearing again the tune to which they had danced and drowsily on the threshold of dreams she could feel Randy's arm around her.

CHAPTER TWELVE

TOWARD DAWN she slept fitfully, waking at intervals to consult the illuminated dial of the small traveling clock on her bedside table. Overanxious to be on time for her meeting with Lanty, she was dressing by six o'clock, trying to ignore the sinking feeling within her. In the cold light of morning the expedition seemed even more rash than last night. Lanty and his friend were up to no good. If they knew something about the missing will they ought to tell the police; instead of which they were going to use their information, it seemed, to drive some bargain with her concerning the disposal of the Osborne lands. How would they feel when they discovered that she was out to get their information without making any concession in return? Away on a lonely island lost in that vast lake, she would be entirely at their mercy. A wave of cold panic swept over her so that she stood suddenly halted in the act of brushing her hair. In the mirror she could see her face ashy white, her eyes dark and enormous. Just for an instant the impulse to go to Randy and tell him the whole queer story was almost overpowering. Couldn't he corner Lanty, force him by questioning to tell what he knew of the will? But even while she asked herself this facile question, she knew she was merely wasting her time. A cornered Lanty would be obstinate and altogether useless, and his slick Irish wits would provide any number of misleading answers to questions he wanted to evade. No, the only way to get anything out of Lanty and his friend was to appear to play their game with them. *And I'm the only person who can do it,* Cathleen thought unhappily. Because they thought she might be of some use to them they had decided to take her into their confidence. Well she must play up that confidence for all it was worth.

Hurrying downstairs on legs that were not altogether steady, she found a fresh complication awaiting her. There in the hall was Mollie, already up and fully dressed. She looked pale and worried and greeted Cathleen with obvious relief. "Oh, Cathleen, you are early this morning. I'm so glad. I was dying to come and rouse you, but didn't have the nerve after our late night. Yo-Yo is lost!" The last words were spoken in so abysmal a tone that Cathleen found it difficult to express a smile. But Mollie, who had spent a sleepless night worrying over the missing Siamese was in so overwrought a state that it would have been cruel to laugh at her.

"He wasn't anywhere when we got in last night," the little girl went on, "and you know how he always rushes to welcome me home! I've questioned the servants and nobody saw him all day yesterday. He ran out after the dogs in the early morning, remember? And he hasn't been seen since."

"Perhaps he has gone rabbit hunting," Cathleen suggested.

Mollie shook her head. "Even rabbits wouldn't keep him away from home for twenty-four hours. You know how hungry he always is for his meals, turning up on the dot to howl at me until he sees me producing his tin plate. And he has never yet missed a night curled up on the foot of my bed. It was awful without him last night. . . ." Mollie's lower lip trembled ominously. "I'm just going out to ransack the woods . . . he may be caught in a trap." She gulped back something that sounded suspiciously like a sob. "Will you come and help me look for him?"

Cathleen glanced distractedly at the desperate little face lifted to her. This was dreadful! She'd got to shake the child off somehow. Already the clock on the dusty antler-hung wall was pointing to six-thirty. Murmuring something noncommittal she followed Mollie out onto the terrace steps. "We'd better split up—search in different directions," she suggested, hating herself for this two-faced villainy. But she had to keep her rendezvous with Lanty and Mollie mustn't see them meet. "You go up by Doon Hill and I'll take the larch wood," she ordered crisply and Mollie's ready acceptance of the little ruse made her feel more of a villain than ever. As soon as she returned from the island, however, she'd spend the rest of the day if necessary searching for Yo-Yo, she consoled herself, as she hurried along the path to the loch.

Lanty was waiting for her in the shadow of a clump of hydrangeas that concealed also the small outboard motorboat moored to the quay wall. With his coat collar turned up to his ears and a cap pulled down over his eyes, he looked every inch a conspirator. "In with you, miss!" he ordered curtly, jumping into the small craft ahead of her.

"This engine will wake the dead!" Cathleen protested nervously, as he touched the noisy mechanism into life. Mollie, climbing the Doon Hill, would most certainly be startled by the racket. Supposing she were to look down and see them! Cowering nervously below the level of the inadequate gunwale, Cathleen couldn't help pointing out that they must be pretty conspicious from the castle windows. . . .

"So what!" retorted Lanty in the film parlance that matched his gangster setup.

"Only that if you'd wanted to keep this expedition secret it might have been wiser to stick to rowing—at least until we got out of earshot of the land."

"We're going too far for oars. Black Island is a good six miles away and I'm not worried if Mr. Bloomin' Randy Kilmoran does happen to see me setting off in his boat. As long as I've got you here with me and we're on our way, the whole thing is as good as in the bag. What Mr. Blasted Kilmoran thinks about me, or about you, isn't going to matter a tinker's curse by the time we get back to Castle Osborne. We'll have finished with him then as completely as though it was himself, and not just a bit of paper we were going out to Black Island to destroy.''

Cathleen went crimson. Lanty's manner this morning was so offensive that she couldn't help feeling pretty certain there was something more than mere bluster behind it. How dare he speak of Randy like this? Controlling the angry protest that rose to her lips she gave him a cold stare. That odd remark about a bit of paper!

''Your friend out on Black Island has some document in connection with the missing will?'' she hazarded.

''There isn't any friend. I just told you that to kid you along last night in case you started putting two and two together too quickly.'' His blue eyes leered at her in cunning and in triumph. ''Black Island is me own hideout. I've got a poteen still there; I've had it this twelve months or more and no police raid has ever yet caught up on it. Even the police are afraid to go out there on account of the bad name the place has because of the killing that was on it.''

''The killing!'' Cathleen echoed through dry lips.

''A murder,'' Lanty returned with lurid satisfaction. ''One fellow that brained another fellow with a rock a while back and left his body there to rot. It wasn't found for nigh on two years. No one goes near the place anymore because of the curse that is on it.''

Cathleen shivered in the still morning air.

''That's why I hid the will over there,'' Lanty said quietly.

Cathleen caught her breath sharply. ''You have Lady Fitz-Osborne's will!'' she whispered.

Lanty nodded portentously. ''I have it right enough, but we'll see the last of it this morning—when you have signed the little bit of paper I have ready for you. We'll burn the will in the fire of the poteen still—the two of us together, sharing the guilt of it, and sharing the profits. That's the whole story for you now,

Cousin Cathleen; that's why I brought you out here this morning.''

For a moment or two Cathleen sat in stunned silence, but stronger than the shock of Lanty's last words ran a current of sheer jubiliation. *The will existed; Randy's inheritance was safe.* In that first moment of immense relief she could overlook the unpleasant implications of this morning's odd journey and the almost insuperable difficulties that must still be surmounted if she were to get the will out of Lanty's clutches.

''What exactly is it you want me to do, Lanty?'' she asked quietly.

Lounging over the tiller he pushed his cap back on his handsome blond head, and then as though further to establish his air of nonchalance spat lustily over the side of the rapidly moving boat. ''What I want you to do is to play fair with me. I've saved your inheritance for you, haven't I? Well, I want a suitable reward for the job. Castle Osborne and the wide lands that go with it—what's it worth to you?''

Nothing, she wanted to blurt out; nothing at all compared with something else that is far more important! But she bit back the words and gave him what she hoped was a shrewd and conspirational glance. ''You mean you want me to pay you something for handing the will over to me?''

''No,'' he said. ''There's no need for me to hand the will over to you—the will is as good as burned right now. The only reason I'm making you help in its destruction is so that you'll be properly in it with me—partners in crime; see what I mean?'' He laughed unpleasantly. ''Women have dangerous tongues, ye know, but this morning's work should keep yours quiet. You'll burn that will with me standing over you. But before I let you do that you've got to sign a paper making certain parts of the Osborne lands over to me. I want the stretch of peat on the Doon Hill and the arable lands running down from there to Doon crossroads. And I want that new meadow Randy is after making below by the lough.''

Randy's beautiful, Italian ryegrass and clover! Cathleen drew in a sharp breath. ''Is that all?'' she inquired, with an inflection of sarcasm quite lost on the flushed and jubilant Lanty. How sure of himself he was; not a doubt in his mind, but that she would be only too ready to fall in with his plans!

''I'll want five hundred quid in addition,'' he was saying easily. ''In cash, as soon as you get your hands on the capital. I know there'll be a bit of legal delay like, before you are in full possession of the estate. But I'll be content to wait, as long as I have your signature on the little bit of an agreement I've drawn up for you.''

Cathleen digested this in silence. Lanty had certainly worked everything out in clear detail. But why had he taken the will in the first place, long before he had had any idea she was Lady FitzOsborne's granddaughter, and therefore the person he might be expected to consider as the rightful heir? He hated Randy, of course.

''Lanty,'' she asked presently, ''was it because of Mr. Kilmoran that you suppressed the will in the beginning—I mean you couldn't have known I had anything to do with the family the night Lady FitzOsborne died.''

He gave her a long somber look, and loathing smoldered in his eyes. ''That fellow!'' he muttered. ''That upstart! And old Mary Costello always boasting of the way the property was to be left to him, and how I'd have to pull myself together and give up drinking when he became my master. 'It's not just a poor helpless old lady you'll have over you then, but a man who will be after you morning and night; you with your pilfering and slacking and slipping off with you to your poteen making! You won't get away with it so easy when Randy is your boss,' she'd say, taunting me until I was ready to raise me fist to her. Every word of the will then she'd tell me mother and grandmother back home, and how she was one of the witnesses to it.''

"And did they mind the FitzOsborne estate going to a Kilmoran?'' Cathleen asked, holding her breath back because somehow the answer was frightfully important.

"Sure, they didn't mind a bit. They've no spirit, those old women, only saying their prayers and think of heaven, and Mary Costello had them as mesmerized as herself by the grandeur of the Kilmorans—on account of Lady FitzOsborne being one of that blasted clan. In a month of Sundays it wouldn't come into their minds that they had any rights in the property themselves because of Miss Sheila marrying my Uncle Mike. It takes a man to work out that kind of a legal situation,'' said Lanty, puffing out his chest.

"Yes, I suppose so,'' Cathleen agreed, conscious of a wave of relief. No matter how tricky Lanty had been, the Costello women were not involved.

"And how did you actually get hold of the will?'' she was asking presently.

Lanty puffed out his chest a little farther. "By using me wits,'' he answered tersely, and might have left it at that if his vanity hadn't urged him on. Cathleen couldn't fail to be impressed, he felt, when she heard the story. He had, it seemed, been sent to the sickroom to tend the fire on the night of Lady FitzOsborne's fatal seizure, and finding himself for a moment alone in the room with the sick woman, had thought at once of the notorious document that had already given him so much heartburning. "I wasn't rightly sure I would be able to get a hold of it,'' he went on, "but I knew it was in the safe by the bed it was usually kept. I took one look at the old one breathing her last on the bed, put me hand into the safe—which wasn't locked by the grace of God—and pulled out a fistful of papers, stuffing them into me jacket pocket. Then back with me to the hearth, letting on to be sweeping up the ashes as me Aunt Mary and the doctor walked into the room.'' He chuckled to himself as though he found the macabre recollection vastly entertaining.

''And why didn't you destroy the will right away?'' Cathleen asked.

A look of cunning came over Lanty's face. ''I didn't like to at first. I wanted to have a good read of it and get the proper hand of it. There's no use being in a hurry over a thing like that. So I stole out of the house the minute herself was dead, and got into the rowboat and away with me to Black Island, where I hid the whole of the papers until such time as I had leisure to go reading them.''

''Then you rowed back again,'' Cathleen said, ''and I met you coming into the shore about noon. Remember?''

Lanty gave her a companionable grin. ''I do, indeed, and the fright I got when I saw you! I hadn't a notion then who you really were; it wasn't until a couple of days later Aunt Mary began rambling to herself about the look you had of Miss Sheila. After that I used to be listening to that lawyer fellow, Philligan, talking about Miss Sheila's rights being uppermost so long as there was no other will. Biding my time I was until the day I heard yourself declaring there in the library that you were Miss Sheila's daughter. I knew then I did right to hold back the will—and there I was working out in my mind how grateful you would be to me once you had the proof I had saved your inheritance for you . . . not forgetting all I might expect to get out of the transaction meself!'' The calculating look he gave her made her feel slightly sick.

They were far out of the lough now, the shore a blur of blue hills shrouded in morning mist. The helplessness of her position struck Cathleen afresh, as she contemplated the utter solitude surrounding them; this vast emptiness of water and sky, the silence unbroken save for the ripple of the boat's wash, the whir of wings as a covey of wild duck rose startled before them. How would Lanty react when he found that she had no intention of falling in with his evil plans? When he discovered that he had not after all provided himself with an accomplice—but a hostile witness! With a suppressed shiver she saw that they were heading now for a small desolate island.

"Is this it?" she asked unsteadily.

"This is Black Island," Lanty said, and a few moments later she was stepping out of the boat onto a shelving beach littered with the broken stems of dried rushes. Birds rose screaming at their intrusion, mallard and coot and gulls. The rushing of their wings and their raucous cries filled the air, so that Cathleen could hardly hear Lanty saying, "Show you how far out of the world we are! Not a soul but myself ever disturbs them."

He was leading her over the rough ground as he spoke, his manner hurried and excited. Rocks towered before them and beyond the rocks there was a thick plantation of stunted trees rising from a tangle of blackberry bushes and sloe through which Lanty pushed his way, holding the briars back to allow Cathleen to follow him. Presently the ground cleared a little, and there was the entry to a rough cave in the rocks. "It is here I have my poteen still," Lanty confided, and disappeared into the dark entry, returning with an old tin box in his hand. "I have a bit of a fireplace in there where I keep a fire of turf for the distilling," he confided. "We can burn the will in it when you have signed this paper." Opening the tin box he drew forth a sheet of foolscap that he handed to Cathleen with an air of pride. "The little agreement between ourselves I drew up for ye," he announced. An ill-written scrawl confronted her, the words dancing before her eyes as she glanced at them.

"Now show me the will," she said. Her throat was tight, her mouth dry as she took the second document produced from the tin box. It was very short and simple, bequeathing Castle Osborne and all lands and monies according thereto to Randal Kilmoran. Lady FitzOsborne's signature had been witnessed by Mary Costello and Philligan, the solicitor.

Drawing in a deep shaken breath, Cathleen raised her eyes from the page. "Let me take this—and your agreement home and consider them," she suggested, without much hope that Lanty could be so easily caught.

He grinned. "I'm not such a fool as you take me for, my good girl! You'll sign the paper promising me my field and my five hundred pounds before we leave this island. And we'll burn Mr. Randy's fortune here and now...." His hand shot out and before she had realized his purpose he had snatched the will back from her.

With a suffocating sensation she looked at the wall of trees surrounding them. She could feel her panic rising, swamping all caution. There wasn't time for caution with Lanty already turning toward the cave and the waiting fire with the will in his hand.

"I'm not signing that agreement you've drawn up, Lanty," she blurted hysterically. "And if you burn Lady FitzOsborne's will I'm going straight to the police when we get back to report you."

She could see the shock of this announcement hitting him like a hammer blow over the heart. His ruddy face turned a mottled color and his eyes went glazed. There was a long and dreadful silence before he was able to speak. "You're joking!" he brought out then, in a choked voice.

"I'm not joking."

"You mean you're ready to let the chance of owning Castle Osborne slip away from you for the sake of doing me down?"

"Not for the sake of doing you down—but because I'd rather die than be party to a fraud of this kind."

Lanty stared at her in blankest bewilderment. Clearly, it had never for one moment occurred to him that she might take this attitude, that anyone in their right senses *could* take it. To let a great property like Castle Osborne slip away into the hands of an interloper without lifting one finger to save it! She must be mad.

"We can't do it, Lanty," she urged. "It's criminal to destroy wills. And even if we weren't found out," she added on a flash of inspiration, remembering how powerful superstition could be, "it wouldn't bring us any luck to go against the wishes of the dead. Listen to me now and I'll make a deal with you. Give me the will and I'll pretend I found it somewhere in the castle. I promise you solemnly that I won't betray the part you had in its disappearance."

Anger flared in his eyes. "You're not right in the head," he said crudely. "If you think I'm going to stand aside and see Kilmoran lording it over Castle Osborne, you're mistaken."

"And if you think I'm going to join you in your wicked schemings, *you're* mistaken," Cathleen returned hotly. "Give me the will now and be sensible, Lanty. Forget you ever had it in your possession—and I'll forget it, too. I can't say fairer then that."

"You can say a lot fairer," Lanty shouted, his face purple with rage. "And by heaven you're not getting off this island until you do!" He turned then, and, almost before she had realized his purpose, he had crashed through the undergrowth and left her.

"Lanty!" she called breathlessly. "Lanty!" But it was a slow business working her way through the clinging thorny briars, and long before she had reached the little strand she heard the motor outboard starting up. By the time she got to the water's edge the boat was already far out on the waters.

"Lanty!" she called frantically, "come back here at once and take me off!"

He waved an airy hand and laughed unpleasantly. "I'm not taking you off, my girl, until you sign our little agreement. Maybe I'll come back in the morning," he shouted across the widening distance. "We'll see what a night with the ghosts of Black Island will do to bring you to your senses."

Incredulously, Cathleen watched the boat until it was no more than a speck on the lonely stretch of water. "Tomorrow morning!" she whispered to herself, then weakly her knees seemed to dissolve and she sank to the ground.

Afterward when she looked back on it, the details of that long day on Black Island were always a little blurred, like a bad dream remembered in terms that had no relation to reality. The hot sun beating on the little foreshore and the way the light danced upon the empty expanse of water, so that her eyes were burning in her head as she watched hour after hour for some sign of a passing craft to which she might signal. Only that there were never any passing craft. Lanty had evidently chosen his hideout right away from the more popular sailing routes.

She couldn't remember just when it was the utter silence began to get her down, and the way the birds came back one by one, hopping around among the reeds, going about their affairs as though she were already dead, lying there. It must have been around about dusk that her mind slipped into a kind of dizziness of exhaustion, and she began to see wavering forms among the bushes—gaunt terrible men with stones in their hands and murder in their eyes. There was a body, then, it seemed to her overwrought nerves a gashed and dreadful corpse stretched out on the rocks not far from her. But she knew all this was imagination, and that she must not give in to it. The dizziness came from being hungry, so did the fantasies of a murder over and done with years before. Disconnected phrases kept repeating themselves in her head. "I am a young fellow that ran out of my land and means." Randy's unfortunate song. Snatches of the ballads she had heard at the Ceilidh last night. "Oh the Shannon's tide runs dark and wide between my love and me," and something about a little red fox with his two little ears together. And all the time she could hear the throbbing of the tune the radio was playing while she had danced with Randy's arms around her.

When the twilight thickened into a pale grayness that was

never quite dark, it grew bitterly cold, and the cold made her feel more sensible, though at the same time more acutely miserable. The little rustlings and stirrings in the undergrowth behind her were terrifying if she let herself think about them, and it must have been somewhere around midnight that she had the idea of lighting a fire. There was a cigarette lighter in her handbag, and when she had piled some of the dried rushes together and set them ablaze, she began to be more hopeful. The warmth was so comforting, and surely, even on the mainland six miles away, her bonfire might attract attention if she made it big enough. But in the end the fire wasn't much of a success, the dried rushes burned out so quickly, and it was too difficult in the darkness to find a sufficient supply. Lying down by the embers with her head on her arm she drifted into an uneasy doze, haunted by the thought of Lanty's return—for it would bring no real easing to a situation now truly desperate. Oh, how foolish she had been to come here! She was not nearer getting hold of the will than she had ever been, and Lanty's dilemma when he found she still held out against him would be serious indeed. To take her back to the mainland would be to incriminate himself utterly—and he would never do that. What, then, could he do? A Lanty maddened by the prospect of exposure! She was fully awake then with the sudden realization of the true nature of her plight. In anguish it came to her that the elements that could make a murder once more haunted this cursed spot—rage and the blind terror of guilt—and a shot in the darkness.

When she heard the distant throbbing of the little outboard motor, she lay frozen in cold and mindless fear, her face pressed into her hands. Like a trapped animal she waited, listening with senses desperately alert to the grating of a keel on the stony beach close to her. Heavy footsteps crunched over the brittle reeds and rigidly she held herself, aware of the man who now stood over her. She could hear his breath drawn sharply, the little exclamation spoken softly and in horror as his hand came down on her shoulder and at the sound of his voice unbearable relief flooded her. Black dizziness threatened as the dreadful tension snapped, but she could feel the strong arms lifting her up, holding her close.

"Randy!" she whispered incredulously. "Oh, Randy! Thank God you've got here!"

CHAPTER THIRTEEN

AFTER THAT everything was a little vague to Cathleen for a few moments. The relief of seeing Randy was so overwhelming that it made her feel quite weak and dizzy; so that it wasn't easy to concentrate on the questions he was pouring out. Rather indignant questions they sounded, though the face bending over her was haggard with concern in the red glow of the dying fire.

"I'm all right," she gasped out presently, forcing herself to sit up. "It's only that I was half-asleep when you turned up, and I thought you were . . . somebody else and was frightened. Besides it's been dreadfully cold here all night." Her teeth were chattering as she spoke, and with a quick protective movement Randy threw off his tweed jacket and wrapped it around her shoulders.

"Well, let's leave the explanations just now—they can wait," he muttered in a baffled way. "Just lie there and relax while I get this fire going again to warm you up a bit before we start back."

Snuggling down in the rough tweed coat, Cathleen felt drowsy and safe. Being free of the fear of Lanty was such bliss that she didn't want to think of anything else. Presently she'd have to decide just how much Randy ought to be told of the adventures of the past strange twenty-four hours. Just now she couldn't even bother to wonder how he had discovered she was marooned on Black Island. Huddled in the tweed coat, she watched him working over the fire.

In the shadowy half-light he looked very large and very much in earnest, as though he were unaccustomed to lighting fires and it was taking a great deal of concentration. The bright light from the flames beginning to lick at the newly piled driftwood did interesting things to his face, emphasizing the long lean line of the jaw, the strong bones of the dogged chin, deepening the lines of weariness around his eyes. In the shadow thrown by the leaping lights his lashes seemed ridiculously long—so that in spite of the lines of weariness he looked very young and somehow vulnerable.

He has unhappy eyes, she thought, *and a mouth that can show too easily when he is hurt.* The muddle about the will had hurt him a great deal. And with a stab of pain Cathleen remembered that it was a muddle that still persisted. She had come to the island full of foolish hopes, but she had failed utterly. Lanty had gone away with the precious document in his pocket. Perhaps in his panic he had already destroyed it! It was the obvious thing for him to do if he felt himself cornered. With the will destroyed he could deny any accusations she might bring against him. After all, there would only be her word against his to prove the troublesome thing had ever existed. With a sigh of sheer misery she buried her face in the tweed coat. It smelled comfortably of heather and peat smoke and tobacco. If only she had managed her interview with Lanty more cleverly! But she had panicked . . . shouted at him. It was almost unbearable to think that she had actually had her hands on the will, only to allow it to be snatched away from her again.

Randy, still bending over the uncertain fire, gave her an anxious glance.

"What are you sighing about? You aren't going to faint again, are you?" he asked nervously.

"I never faint," Cathleen declared stoutly. "When I went a bit light-headed just now it was simply because I'm hungry. I haven't had anything to eat since yesterday—or the day before yesterday to be exact, when we had dinner at the Angler's."

Randy straightened in a startled way. "You mean you've been stuck on this island all these hours without any grub?"

"Well, I didn't find any breadfruit trees or date palms," Cathleen said with a warm smile. "Not as much as a solitary mushroom. I'm not a very successful Robinson Crusoe."

"You weren't picnicking then? You came over here without a luncheon basket?"

"I came without as much as a bite of breakfast inside me!"

"In heaven's name why?" Randy began impatiently, and broke off with a startled glance at her pale face. "All right—don't bother to answer questions just now. There's a flask of brandy in the locker of the boat . . . I ought to have thought of that sooner." He was off into the darkness beyond the firelight then, and she could hear him hurrying over the stones of the beach. A dizzy but peaceful drowsiness possessed her as the warmth from the fire seeped through her chilled bones, and in a moment Randy returned, not only with the brandy that she sipped from the neck of the bottle in distaste, but with a tin of biscuits he'd discovered stowed away among the fishing gear.

The raw brandy was burning and horrible, making her choke, but almost at once she could feel its reviving effect. Everything seemed suddenly more vivid and real and she wasn't dizzy anymore. The biscuits, she said, tasted better than anything she had ever eaten in her life. "I was almost reduced to gnawing at the stems of the dried rushes," she confessed with a laugh. "If I'd only known what was before me this morning when I left Castle Osborne, I could at least have put a slab of chocolate in my pocket."

"Mollie said you started off about six-thirty . . . with the idea of helping her to search for Yo-Yo," Randy shot at her inquiringly. "At least that was what she'd understood. Then she saw you setting off across the loch in the small outboard with Lanty Conor."

"I know," Cathleen admitted evasively. "It must have seemed a bit queer to her."

"It has been a queer day altogether," Randy said, in the voice of a man who has reached a state of resignation where almost any improbability can be accepted. "I seem to have done nothing but go from one rescue party to another. First it was Mollie. Out on the hunt for Yo-Yo she got herself caught in a boghole in Doonside and had the fright of her life, poor kid. Luckily Finnerty the cowman heard her screams and he darted down to the castle for me. We took boards and ropes. . . ."

"Poor Mollie!" Cathleen whispered in horror. "Do you mean she was actually sinking in that terrible bog mud?"

"I don't think she'd have sunk very far. It wasn't a deep hole. But she was sucked in almost up to her knees and couldn't free herself. If it had happened in the darkness she might have been held there all night. As it was . . . there were no bones broken and as soon as she got home and had a hot bath she was none the worse. Only, there was Yo-Yo still to be accounted for. We spent the rest of the morning ransacking the mountains for him, digging out foxes' earths and heaven knows what, with Mollie growing more and more tearful every minute. . . ."

"But you did find him?" Cathleen threw in, unable to wait for the leisurely climax.

"We found him around about teatime, as happy as a lark in the cottage of old Dan the gardener, who adores him. I don't know why we didn't think of looking there for him in the first place. He'd moved over to Dan's yesterday, it seems, when Mollie went out on that cross-country trek with you. He hates being left alone, as you know, and Dan was only too glad to give him a welcome. There he was hunting mice in Dan's attic. . . . It was only after we'd brought him home that it began to dawn on us it was a bit queer you hadn't shown up. When dinnertime came around and you still hadn't appeared, it began to look a bit odd. Especially as Lanty Conor, with whom you were last seen, was reported to be getting himself roaring drunk at Danahan's shebeen. The boat he'd taken you out in was found moored to the quay below the larch wood, but you were missing. It wasn't so good!'' Something in the aggrieved way he looked at her as he said this made her heart give a foolish lurch.

''So I went hotfoot down to Danahan's,'' he was continuing, ''and took Lanty Conor by the scruff of the neck and demanded to know what he'd done with you.''

''What did he say?'' Cathleen asked her eyes wide at the thought of Lanty's dilemma. So awkward a question and Randy's sinewy hand at his throat! Lanty was a big man, but he wasn't on the same scale as the broad-shouldered, muscular Randy.

''He said he'd taken you fishing and that you were casting for bream in the neighborhood of the Doorush Islands and that you were using a bit of a dinghy you'd hired from some boatman at Osbornestown quay. He wasn't sure of the name of the boatman when I questioned him, but he built up a most circumstantial story about the habit bream have of rising to feed only at dawn, and how you'd said you'd stay around Doorush all night in the hopes of making a good catch.''

''Me that never had a fishing rod in my hand and wouldn't know a bream from a herring!'' Cathleen marveled.

''That thought did occur to me,'' Randy admitted dryly. ''But Lanty was too drunk to be anything but obstinate and argumentative—sticking to his silly story until I punched him on the jaw and he passed out.''

Cathleen shivered at the mental picture conjured up. Randy reduced to acts of violence in a public house! ''I'm so sorry,'' she offered apologetically. ''I'd no idea you would be so worried about me.''

''Well, how would you expect me to feel?'' he countered

gruffly. "After all, you are my guest and I'm more or less responsible for you to your people . . . your fiancé. . . ."

"If you mean Len Cranton," Cathleen threw in a little too hurriedly and breathlessly, "he is *not* my fiancé. . . ." Eagerly she waited for effect of this announcement, but Randy ignoring it completely seemed all at once immensely absorbed with the rebuilding of the fire, so that the spate of confidences died on her lips. Maybe it wasn't quite the moment to enter into the history of her purely neighborly association with the boy who had lived next door to her in Petunia Road. A boy who had traveled some hundreds of miles to see her the other day; who had held her in his arms and kissed her more or less under Randy's nose! A wave of utter hopelessness swept over her as she heard Randy say coldly, "Next time you decide to go off for a day's outing with a skunk like Lanty Conor, I wish you would at least mention it to me."

It's no use, she thought, *he doesn't really care whether Len is my fiancé or not.* That he had himself once held her in his arms and kissed her had probably retreated from his mind into some limbo of half-forgotten mildly amorous encounters. A girl he had flirted with briefly . . . until she had rounded upon him with an entirely unjust accusation of self-interest that had, no doubt, hurt his pride a great deal.

"I couldn't tell you I was going out with Lanty. It was a . . . particularly secret matter that was involved," she began haltingly, hating the inconclusive story that now she must unfold. If only she had managed to keep the will in her grasp! As it was, the whole enterprise was going to sound absolutely fatuous.

"If it wasn't that I happened to run into Patsy Shane at Danahan's," Randy interrupted "you'd have stayed here until you died of hunger, I suppose."

"Patsy Shane?" Cathleen echoed blankly.

"Patsy is a turf cutter from the other side of the lough. He was in Danahan's the second time I went there . . . meaning to have another go at Lanty if I could find him. But he'd cleared off. I'd been out to Doorush, you see, half hoping that there might have been some word of truth in his rigmarole. But there was no sign of you in that quarter, and anyway, it was dark by then and looking for a dinghy in the dark on thirty miles of open water seemed to me somewhat a waste of time. Danahan's was closed, of course—it was almost midnight—but Patsy was having an illegal booze in the snug and poured out a long spiel about a ghost he'd seen on Black island when he was crossing the lough in the dusk with a load of turf. Some chap that was murdered here a couple of years ago. A body stretched out on the stones of the shore, was how Patsy described it. He was pretty shaken."

"He passed here!" Cathleen exclaimed in amazement. "And I never saw him. It must have been before I lighted my fire. I might even have been asleep."

"I wasn't so quick on the uptake myself," Randy admitted. "It wasn't until after I'd got back to the castle that it dawned on me Patsy's story could possibly have a grain of fact in it—that it might be yourself he saw on Black Island. . . ."

"A body stretched out on the stones!" Cathleen put in with a shudder.

Randy gave her a hollow sort of look and his laugh wasn't altogether convincing. "I hadn't got quite to the stage of search-party nerves where one starts looking for bodies! Not that I was particularly happy about you." He broke off short. Just what horrors had gone through his mind on that long journey across the lough he would keep to himself. "I knew you must be in *some* kind of jam," he went on quietly. "If you'd got as far as Black Island in a dinghy there wouldn't be much chance of your getting back, once night had overtaken you. Seems my guess was about right." He stood up abruptly. "And now what about getting you home? You look absolutely done in. We can tow your dinghy—or leave it here till some other time.''

"There isn't any dinghy,'' Cathleen said. "Lanty Conor marooned me here.'' Drawing the tweed jacket closer around her she sat up with a shiver. Behind the eastern wall of the hills the sky was paling, and it was the chill wind of dawn that now ruffled the lake waters. "Listen, Randy!'' Her voice was tense. "We can't go home, yet. I've been thinking it out, while you've been talking. We've got to stay here. Because Lanty Conor is probably coming back, and the way we handle him when he does come back is going to decide something of the utmost importance . . . to both of us.'' Even as she spoke there came a faint throbbing; an outboard motor far away sending its echoes across the miles of shadowed water. . . .

"You see,'' she whispered, "he has, or ought to have Lady FitzOsborne's missing will in his pocket.''

Randy stared at her. "Lady FitzOsborne's will!'' he echoed in stupefaction.

Cathleen peered desperately across the lough to the point where the throbbing seemed to be located, each moment growing louder. Drawing in a deep breath she embarked on her story. She told it very badly—there was so little time! But Randy had to understand something of the situation if he was to be of any real help. Stolen wills, blackmailing demands, her nightmare evening with Lanty at the Angler's when all she had really gathered was that he knew something about the missing will and would disclose more of its mystery if she accompanied him to Black Island; in the coldly growing light of that chill and overcast morning it all sounded so improbable and crazy!

When she ended this odd recital, Randy was looking down at her with all the incredulity in his gray eyes that she had expected.

"Didn't it occur to you that it was a pretty risky thing to go off alone with a tough like Lanty Conor on a wild goose chase that could have had pretty shady implications?'' he asked at last, his voice gruff and very stern.

Cathleen nodded. ''I wasn't exactly happy about it.''

''You could have . . . let me handle it?''

''But that's just what I couldn't do! One word from you to Lanty would have ruined everything. You were the chief victim of the plot, you see. He didn't want you to get Osborne. That's why he'd stolen the will in the first place.'' She heard Randy's muffled exclamations of astonishment as she hurried on with the rest of the sordid little story.

''And you actually saw the will!'' he marveled, when she had finished.

''I had it in my hand! Only to have it snatched away from me again.'' Her voice choked with misery. ''I had to watch him go off with it in his pocket in such a rage that he may, by now, have done anything with it! Only that I'm counting he *will* bring it back. He's got everything to gain by holding on to it, in the hopes that I will by this time be frightened into signing the agreement to hand him over some of the land and the five hundred pounds he wants.''

But Randy didn't appear to be listening very closely anymore. In the wan early dawn his young face looked drawn and tired and yet curiously lit up, his gray eyes very dark and bright. He said, ''You did all this . . . risked coming out here with a man mad enough and wicked enough to have done you serious harm . . . simply in order to do yourself out of Castle Osborne and hand it over to me!''

If only he didn't have such ridiculously long eyelashes! Cathleen was thinking with crazy irrelevance. If only he wouldn't go on looking at her in that rapt and ardent fashion. An Irishman's blandishing look for a girl who was no more to him than a guest for whom he happened to be responsible, and now toward whom he had a reason for some gratitude.

"You risked your life for me, Cathleen. Why?" he whispered.

"My British love of fair play I expect," she returned, with a casual shrug. "I told you all along I hated the idea of being saddled with Castle Osborne."

Randy turned away quickly and she couldn't see his face anymore. "I'd better set about shoving that boat of mine out of view," he said in a flat tone. His shoulders seemed to sag as he went slowly over the stony beach and she could see his short-sleeved tennis shirt blown out by the chill dawn wind. *He ought to have his jacket on,* she thought, and there were sudden tears in her eyes. They dropped slowly down onto the tweed lapels huddled up under her chin. She couldn't have told just why she was crying, only that she was desperately tired with the long strain she had endured and the wind was cold and the loch looked steely gray and inimical under the colorless, heartless sky. The sound of the outboard motor was growing more definite now, though there still wasn't any sight of it. Progress would be slow this morning, with the current running strongly under that freshening wind and the white tops beginning to curl on waves that would have done credit to an open sea.

When Randy returned after hiding his boat securely, drops of cold rain were splashing down on the flat stones of the beach. But in spite of this, Cathleen took the tweed jacket from her shoulders and insisted upon Randy wearing it. "You have to take it, anyhow, rain or no rain," she pointed out. "It wouldn't be very clever of us to let Lanty arrive and find me wearing your coat, would it?"

They could just see the black speck that was Lanty's boat now appearing and disappearing in the troughs of the waves. In hurried tones they made their final arrangements. Randy was to hide in the thick hazel bushes that grew close to the beach, and when Lanty landed Cathleen would pretend that she had been beaten by her hours of solitude. She would sign the paper, agree to burn the will. "As soon as I have it in my hand you must rush out of your hiding place," she planned feverishly. She was so excited now that she could feel herself trembling. Everything she had worked for would sort itself out in the next few minutes. Anxious, voiceless little prayers filled her heart, so that she couldn't really listen to Randy saying he hated the idea of hiding in the bushes. Supposing Lanty were to turn violent, he was pointing out.

"He won't," Cathleen argued. "There'll be no need for violence. He'll think he is getting everything his own way. Please, Randy, *go*!" Her two hands were pressed against his tweed shoulders, pushing him away in her urgency, and suddenly he had caught her wrists holding her there imprisoned against him, his gray eyes blazing down at her. He did not speak, just held her there looking down at her with that curious, almost angry intensity, while the rain fell coldly on her upturned face.

Then as abruptly as he had taken her hands he dropped them, and turning went crashing into the thick hazel bushes. Only just in time! For with every moment the daylight was strengthening and the outboard motorboat was now clearly in view. In the short interval that must still elapse before Lanty beached, Cathleen busied herself putting fresh fuel on the dying fire, her chief prop, for it was here she would pretend she was going to burn the will. It wasn't very easy to keep the fire going brightly with the rain hissing down into the hot embers, and all the time she had to control the urge to look over at the spot in the hazel bushes where Randy was concealed. She must remember not to look at the bushes at all when Lanty was with her . . . she must be really careful and clever this time. Leaning over the fire, her head swam with sleepiness and fatigue, and she was horribly nervous in case anything should go wrong.

Then all at once Lanty was close inshore beaching his boat recklessly on a white-crested wave, so that it seemed to smash against the stony landing ground. He was pretty drunk, she saw with a shudder, and all ready to hector her as he swaggered across the stones.

Haltingly she began the little speech of capitulation she had prepared for him, and heard him laugh in triumph. So she had found her night of solitude too much for her, he exulted unpleasantly. "I thought you'd see reason if I gave you time to think," he offered with a smug and self-satisfied leer. "And there'll be no bother about your absence. I've covered that up all right, telling that monkey, Kilmoran, that you were out for a spot of dawn casting, fishing for bream. Hit me on the jaw he did, the bad-tempered ape! Bad cess to him! Wait till I get my two hands on him. . . ."

Cathleen was certain she heard the hazel bushes quiver indignantly at this, and said hurriedly, "Have you got the will there, Lanty? Give it me now and I'll throw it on the fire."

Holding her breath back in an agony of suspense, she waited for his reply. With maddening deliberation he groped in his pockets, and finally produced the folded sheet of parchment. Eagerly Cathleen put out her hand. "Easy now!" Lanty warned. "There's the little matter of the paper you have to sign for myself before we go any further."

With a drunken grin he handed her the ill-scrawled sheet, setting forth his blackmailing terms, and a stub of indelible pencil that she took in unsteady fingers; signing her name while he looked over her shoulder, blowing porter fumes into her face.

Then before she could stop him, with a stunned sense of horror, she saw him fling the folded will into the heart of the fire. There was no time to think. Her hands seemed to act of their own accord, plunging into the leaping flames. She heard Lanty's shout of protest as he leaped toward her. There was just time to be aware of the crashing apart of hazel bushes as Randy emerged, when she felt a stinging blow on the side of her head and everything went dark.

CHAPTER FOURTEEN

A WEEK LATER, in the rosy hour of sunset, Cathleen and Randy stood by the wall of the new meadow looking at the pedigree Herefords knee-deep in the rich clover. The richness of high summer was all around them, a bloom of color laid over the rough land. On the rolling bogs the heather spilled ripe as wine, and every ditch under the toppling stone walls blossomed with creamy meadowsweet and purple loosestrife. Randy's face wore a contented, contemplative expression as he chewed on a stem of ryegrass. The kind of look, Cathleen reflected wistfully that always comes to him when he is thinking about cattle! Covertly she studied the ruggedly handsome profile, as though she tried to learn its lines by heart; the strong line of the nose, the jutting obstinate chin—that deceptive hint of sweetness about the well-cut mouth. As superficial perhaps as the charming turns of speech it could offer to a hungry heart.

During the days that had elapsed since the dramatic events on Black Island, his constant concern for her, his warm gratitude, his eloquently professed admiration for her pluck had dazzled her senses, so that it had been easy enough at first to evade the emptiness that lay behind it all. But suddenly this evening there could be no more evasion and Cathleen's blue eyes under their smudge of dark lashes held a glitter of pain as they took in the details of the tranquil scene she must so soon leave behind. Tomorrow she was going home, and Randy didn't seem to care . . . in spite of his kindly protestations—those glibly spoken phrases that could hurt so much! "But you can't really be leaving us, Cathleen; it doesn't make sense! After all, you're a FitzOsborne *and* a Kilmoran, you've much more claim to the old place than I have myself!'' Castle Osborne, he had emphasized in various degrees of casual good nature was her home . . . she must return to it whenever she felt like visiting it.

When I'm not typing Mr. Gilmer's letters eight hours a day, Cathleen thought, blinking the tears back. Holidays for the world's workers come around so seldom; at the most optimistic estimate it would be a whole year before she could hope to find herself standing once more on the slope of Doon, with the lough spread like a sapphire shield at her feet. And in the end, most probably, she would not have the courage to return at all. What point would there be in returning to this pleasant cousinly atmosphere that could wound so deeply? And what, in heaven's name, she asked herself suddenly, bitterly, as she stood by Randy's side in the sunset glow, had made her imagine there could ever be anything but the mildest of friendship between herself and this self-sufficient kinsman of hers? A kiss in the dark, a dance that had been all heaven, a scatter of the poetically turned phrases any Irishman might have uttered to any pretty girl; why should she have read into these slender tokens a meaning that had never been intended? And what craziness was it that made her, even now, find in the gray eyes that looked down at her an echo of the pain that rent her heart? In the silence that fell between them her pulse pounded nervously and she could feel the color running into her cheeks.

''I'd no idea Herefords were such funny-looking cows,'' she blurted, turning away from that too compelling glance to survey, through a dazzle of tears, the squat chestnut-colored beasts grazing the other side of the low wall. ''When you talked of buying them I thought they would be quite different—graceful and thoroughbred in appearance, like Jerseys. But with their short legs and big white faces they look exactly like circus clowns.'' Running on about Herefords wildly—not caring what she said, only that anything was better than to stand there and let the tears roll down her cheeks.

"Not *cows*, please!" Randy corrected patiently. "Bullocks with beautiful wide backs and thick short haunches—the perfect quick-growing meat producer."

"I . . . hate to think of that part of it," Cathleen faltered. "They look so happy there in the clover, poor things. I'd never make a successful farmer's wife," she ended unthinkingly.

"So I've gathered!" Randy returned in a tight, hard voice, and as they walked on, climbing the slope of Doon, he switched savagely with his stick at the rank grass in their path.

"Petunia Road," he shot at her presently, "a nice little suburban villa and a nice suburban husband . . . that's about your mark, isn't it? A combination much easier to handle than a rambling Irish Castle lost in a wilderness of bog. . . ."

"No," Cathleen answered quietly. "And if you mean Len Cranton, I . . . I'm not marrying Len." Not that it mattered to Randy whom she might marry or not marry, but some instinct of tidiness and truth in her soul made her determined all at once to get at least this much about her life straight in Randy's mind.

"He ought not to have come over last week," she went on dully. "It was . . . presumptuous of him." For a moment she hesitated over the too portentious word, then hurried on. "I mean he knows it is all hopeless; I've told him so many times, and rushing over like that simply because of all the fuss about my inheriting the castle . . . ."

"Just another gold digger, I suppose," Randy put in quietly. "You haven't been very lucky with your boyfriends, have you?"

Cathleen went crimson. "Randy," she said, in a small shamed voice, "I didn't . . . ever really believe you were . . . a gold digger. But I don't suppose there's any way of convincing you . . . now. It's all so much too late and you've . . . Castle Osborne."

"Yes," he agreed in a flat tired voice, "I've got Castle Osborne. Looks good tonight, doesn't it?"

Halting on the high slopes of Doon they turned to survey the scene spread out beneath them; hills and lough and wild, lush lands all bathed in sunset gold, the dusky blur of the wooded valley from which in arrogance the turrets of the old castle arose. All Randy's now, as far as the eye could see, made safe for him by a fold of scorched parchment snatched from a fire by hands that still bore the cruel mark of the leaping flames. That dreadful night on Black Island, how far away it seemed! So much of it for Cathleen blotted out by the blow from Lanty's fist, that had made the happenings of the subsequent twenty-four hours very vague indeed. Randy had brought her back to the castle, a limp and unresisting bundle that had lain heavy in his arms while Lanty, unhindered, made his escape. He hadn't been seen in the district since, and rumor had it he had gone to England to find the profitable factory work and high wages that were tempting so many of his companions from the barren slopes of their Irish hills. This constant flow of emigrants to an alien, rich land! It was all so usual that Lanty's sudden decision to join his fellow exiles hadn't caused the smallest ripple of surprise, not even in his own family circle. And Cathleen had insisted that it should be left that way, had pleaded with passionate intensity that the story of his ill-doings should not be made public, and most certainly not handed over to the police.

It would be so easy to trace him, Randy had argued, for he was bound to carry a travel identity card, and could neither work nor eat in England without registration.

"But I don't want him traced," Cathleen had answered again and again in obstinacy. "Think how horrible it would all be," she had urged, police courts and maybe even an assize trial—all the muddle of the will dragged out in public again, the whole sordid case based on the evidence I would have to give. It would kill me! Oh, Randy, I'd hate it all so! Let it rest the way it is.

People think the will was lost and then simply turned up—the way things do. Let them go on thinking that.''

If he had seemed to give in to her pleading at that hottest moment of their argument, it had simply been because she was still shaken and ill with the shock of that terrible night, her face wan beneath the bandage that swathed her bruised and aching head. There were still bandages on her burned fingers. Perhaps it was the sight of them now as she took her hands from her jacket pocket that made Randy revert with sudden savagery to the subject of the missing Lanty.

In his heartbreakingly gentle way he had taken the wounded hands, holding them lightly, gazing down at them with a look of tight and controlled misery on his handsome face.

Because I hurt myself trying to help him, Cathleen told herself hurriedly. Just that, nothing more—compassion, chivalry, the burden of gratitude and tender concern that had made it so difficult to be with him all these last days. She didn't dare to meet the blazing intensity in his gray eyes as he asked, as he had asked so many times, if the pain in her hands had eased.

''They're wonderfully better, Randy, really! They don't smart at all anymore, and Dr. Mac says I can have the bandages off tomorrow.''

Quite suddenly then, as though in some way he had reached breaking point, Randy was talking again of Lanty's escape. ''Just because you hate the notion of having to give evidence in court,'' he raged, ''you force me into all sorts of silly promises of silence. Cathleen, we've got to come to some more sensible arrangement about all this before you go back to London. It's not even . . . moral to let Conor get away with bare-faced theft, blackmail and a spot of kidnapping thrown in. It's condoning crime.''

With a little sigh, Cathleen withdrew the bandaged hands from his grasp and tucked them back into her pockets—so that the sight of them would no longer upset him. She said steadily and very doggedly, "I can't help it if I *am* condoning crime. I can't be the person to put Lanty Conor in prison. Listen, Randy!" The blue eyes looking up into his grimly set face were bright with earnestness. "My mother married a Costello—and he died; that was old Mrs. Costello's son Michael. Maybe if he hadn't run away with my mother he wouldn't have broken his neck in that drunken steeplechase. Anyway, the Costello family lost one of their men . . . more or less because of a FitzOsborne. I don't want them to suffer again over Lanty, because of me."

Randy bit off an exclamation of impatience and, glancing at the pockets concealing the bandaged hands, said with an obvious effort at control, "Seems a bit farfetched."

"Old Mrs. Costello up at the farm loved my mother," Cathleen went on softly. "I think her's was the only love my mother ever had in childhood, for her own mother didn't want her. It was to Grannie Costello she went for comfort—and Grannie Costello never failed her." The soft voice dropped to a shy whisper. "I think that my mother, if she knew, would want me to be merciful to Lanty now . . . for the old lady's sake. It is something I can do to repay her for all the care and affection poured out on a lonely child."

In the little silence that followed the whispered words, Randy cleared his throat uneasily. "You *would* have to work it all out from some absolutely fantastic angle!" he offered, in a gruff tone of a man emotionally stirred against his will. "Doesn't it ever occur to you to think of your own end of the story—the foul way Lanty behaved to you, the terror and pain you suffered at his hands? Haven't you even one grain of revenge in your unselfish soul?"

"It would hurt his family so terribly if I were to have him sent to prison," she said simply. "His mother, that wonderful dignified Kate, who was Michael's mother . . . and Grannie Costello, who is so kind, so great in her humble way. I couldn't bear to plunge them all into misery and disgrace."

"So Lanty gets off scot-free!" Randy grumbled.

"Not quite. He has had to go into exile . . . away from all this!" The glitter of pain was very bright now in the blue eyes that looked out over the shining golden waters, the folded hills, the rosy fields and little wandering roads. "Maybe he wanted that land he'd schemed for . . . because in his muddled, drunken way he loved it. And quite genuinely he regarded you as an interloper. He really imagined, I think, that the Costellos had some rights in the estate, and half-crazed with poteen as he was . . . the rest would be easy. I don't suppose he realized for a moment the crime he was committing when he concealed what he felt was an unjust will."

Drawing in a shaken breath, Cathleen went on a trifle unsteadily. "A midland factory town after all this, a cheap lodging in some tiny stifling back street. Think of it! Lanty's got his punishment all right . . . an Irishman feeling about his country the way . . . we all do. That hunger for the land that isn't just greed . . . but a passion of devotion that has blossomed into so many heartbroken songs. People who call their country 'Dark Rosaleen,' 'The Dear Dark Rose.' " She broke off, with something like a sob. "Oh, Randy, it's a bewitching land, a soft and lovely siren for whom men have . . . murdered . . . and died. . . ."

He said softly, wonderingly, "You can talk like this . . . feel like this . . . and yet that night on the island you told me Castle Osborne meant nothing to you!"

"Only because it is rightly yours," Cathleen whispered.

"And you wanted me to feel easy about taking it over from you?"

She nodded, her eyes brimming. "I wanted you to feel easy, Randy. It wasn't that I didn't love Castle Osborne and all this. . . ." A small bandaged hand indicated the world that faded beneath them in rose and misty blue—late birds winging over the loch now, a curlew calling in plaintive, piercing sweetness, the muted echoes of a slowly rumbling cart going home along the little white road far down in the valley; the drowsy sounds of evening. "You had asked me," she said unsteadily, "just why I had gone to so much trouble to get the will back for you."

"And you gave me a flippant answer," he said, his hand hard on her shoulder, turning her around, so that it was no longer possible to hide from him the telltale tears that filled her eyes.

Quietly, bravely she looked up at him through the tears. "You wouldn't have cared about the real answer, Randy . . . why should you?"

She could feel the hand on her shoulder tightening now. "What makes you think I wouldn't care?" Randy answered very low. "Don't you realize that I've cared for every least little thing about you ever since a night way back in July, when I watched you sleeping with a Siamese kitten in your arms in a crowded railway carriage?"

Incredulously, through a mist of glory, she looked up at him as he drew her close. Gently his fingertips touched her wet cheeks. "Tears!" he said, "Ah, Cathleen, do not cry! Do not go away from me tomorrow."

"I don't want to go away from you . . . ever," she heard her voice declare in passionate exultation.

"Then what in heaven's name have we been shilly-shallying about all these weeks?"

"I don't know," Cathleen returned with a shaken laugh. "Only that it never occurred to me that you could possibly be interested in an ordinary little nobody like me. I still can't believe it! You seemed so . . . somehow self-sufficient, Randy."

"You're not ordinary. There's a set-apart look about you, like a . . . changeling. I noticed it the moment I saw you at Euston that night; as though you'd strayed out of some other world and had never got over being lonely and lost, though you're too brave to go in for self-pity."

"Maybe it comes from living in Petunia Road," Cathleen said. "Never quite belonging to my family there . . . thinking about my mother, about Ireland. When I got here I didn't feel lost anymore . . . for the first time in my life."

"I had the oddest feeling that night in the train . . . that you were my own flesh and blood," Randy went on musingly. "Maybe it was cousinship asserting itself instinctively—or something a good deal more. When I watched you asleep there were echoes stirring in me . . . like memories. Maybe I'd seen that old painting of Sheila at some time and forgotten it. Or, perhaps it was just that," his voice dropped to a whisper, "that my heart knew you, Cathleen, and cried to me, 'Here she is!' "

"Oh, Randy, what a lovely thing to say!"

"Ah, Cathleen, I love you!" he sighed, and in the twilight she lifted to him her tremulous, wondering face. When he kissed her gently at first and then with rising purpose, it was as though the stars over her head shook with music, and all the world stood still. How long they stayed there on the shadowy hillside she did not know, for time had ceased to matter. And when at last they walked down the path of Doon, hand in hand, their voices were hushed and gentle with content, talking of Castle Osborne now in a drifting way, as though it were something that no longer had power to trouble them.

"It's our home, that's the main thing about it," Randy said, looking down at the gray bulk of the old house, a sprawl of shadow in the gathering night. "When I think how near it came to separating us from one another my blood runs cold. But we can forget all that now."

"Our home!" Cathleen echoed raptly. "Oh, Randy, I've got a feeling that wherever we were together would be home, but I'm glad it's going to be Castle Osborne all the same. I had a feeling I belonged here from the moment I arrived."

"What you really had, though you didn't know it, was a feeling that you belonged to me," Randy amended, with glorious male conceit, and then laughed at himself and stood still to gather her once more into his arms. "I wasn't very clever about helping you to discover it, was I?" he said. "You're going to get a stupid man for a husband, Cathleen; or at least a man who hasn't the faintest notion how to go making himself acceptable to a woman. I've had so little practice, you see."

"I'm glad about that." She laughed up at him in the twilight.

"What you took for self-sufficiency was really a cloak for the most horrible shyness. And then there was all the muddle about the will, with the castle skipping about, belonging to you one day and to me the next so that I never knew quite where I was."

"'I am a young fellow that ran out of my land and means,'" quoted Cathleen mischievously.

"'And placed my affection on one that had gold in store,'" Randy capped, contentedly. "Not a bad scheme, either, if you hadn't made such a fuss about it, it would have saved us a lot of trouble. All the best marriages in Connemara are woven around some bit of property or other. So it's quite in keeping for us to share Castle Osborne . . . just as Mollie has been advising all along. Let's go home and tell her we've laid all the ghosts in both our families. . . ."

"And in our own hearts," whispered Cathleen.

He drew her close. "We won't tell her that bit. That's our own precious secret, darling." And once more he kissed her, and the stars sang in the sky.